MACMILLAN READERS

INTERMEDIATE LEVEL

WILBUR SMITH

River God

Retold by Stephen Colbourn

MACMILLAN

Founding Editor: John Milne

The Macmillan Readers provide a choice of enjoyable reading materials for learners of English. The series is published at six levels – Starter, Beginner, Elementary, Pre-intermediate, Intermediate and Upper.

Level control
Information, structure and vocabulary are controlled to suit the students' ability at each level.

The number of words at each level:

Starter	about 300 basic words
Beginner	about 600 basic words
Elementary	about 1100 basic words
Pre-intermediate	about 1400 basic words
Intermediate	about 1600 basic words
Upper	about 2200 basic words

Vocabulary
Some difficult words and phrases in this book are important for understanding the story. Some of these words are explained in the story and some are shown in the pictures. From Pre-intermediate level upwards, words are marked with a number like this: ...³. These words are explained in the Glossary at the end of the book.

Contents

A Note About the Author

Wilbur Addison Smith was born on 9th January, 1933 in the southern African country which is now called Zambia. At that time, the country was called Northern Rhodesia. It was governed by the British and many British people lived there. Wilbur Smith was educated in South Africa, where he lived for many years.

Wilbur Smith's first book – *When the Lion Feeds* – was published in 1964, and since then he has written more than twenty-five novels. All of them are adventure stories and many of them take place in Africa. Although some of Wilbur Smith's novels are set in the late twentieth century, others are historical novels. The author has written several series of novels about the adventures of families over a long period of time. Wilbur Smith publishes a new novel every two years, and several of his books have been made into successful films.

River God is also part of a series. It is a historical novel which is set in Ancient Egypt, nearly 4000 years ago. It is the first book in a series of three. The second book, *Warlock*, continues the story which is told in this book. The third novel in the series, *The Seventh Scroll*, is set in the present, but it is about the discovery of the papyrus scrolls[1] which tell the stories of the first two books.

A Note About This Story

Although *River God* is not a true story, it includes some historical facts. Most of the general information about Egyptian history in the book is true. Wilbur Smith got the idea for the novel when he heard about the discovery of some ancient papyrus scrolls in Egypt. These records were written by a slave[2]. He had belonged to a woman who had been the wife of a king of Egypt about 3800 years ago. Wilbur Smith used some of the facts that were written in these records and made a story around them.

At the time of the story, Egypt was divided into two kingdoms, each ruled by its own king, or pharaoh. All the towns in the land of Egypt were close to the River Nile. The river was the heart of the country and it was the most important thing in the lives of most of its people. The Nile flooded every year in the spring – the level of the water rose and irrigated the land of Egypt. This was why it was possible to grow food near the river, and why the towns were there. The rest of the country was too dry to grow anything, and few people lived there.

The two Egyptian kingdoms of this period were called Lower Egypt and Upper Egypt. You will see on the map (page 7) that Upper Egypt is in the south and Lower Egypt is in the north, because the river flows 'down' to the sea from south to north.

The Kingdom of Lower Egypt was the area from the Mediterrean coast down to the city of Memphis and a few miles south of that. The Kingdom of Upper Egypt was the area south of Memphis to the First Cataract on the Nile. Cataracts were places where the river was shallow and it flowed very swiftly[3] over the rocks. To the south of the First Cataract was another country, the land of Cush. Today, this area is occupied by Sudan and Ethiopia.

5

About 3800 years ago, Egypt was invaded by people from western Asia. The Egyptians called these people Hyksos. *Hyksos* was simply an Egyptian word for foreign ruler. These invaders probably had better weapons than the Egyptians and a more advanced use of technology. At this time, some people in western Asia had started to use iron for their tools and weapons, rather than bronze. Bronze, which was a softer metal and easier to make things from, had been used for many centuries and the Egyptians still used it.

Another important piece of technology that the Hyksos brought to Egypt was the chariot. Hyksos chariots were pulled by animals that the Egyptians had never seen before – horses. Until the time of the Hyksos invasion, Egyptian soldiers marched and fought on foot. Egyptians sometimes moved heavy objects on sleds pulled by oxen, but the vehicles were slow and they had no wheels. The Hyksos chariots were light and easy to move and the horses could run more swiftly than men. The Egyptians saw that chariots were excellent weapons and very soon they had trained horses and built chariots of their own.

Wilbur Smith makes use of these facts about the changes in technology in his story.

A guide to pronunciation:

Anubis /ə'nu:bɪs/	Duamutef /ˌdʊə'mu:tef/
Imsety /ɪm'seti:/	Isis /'aɪsɪs/
Kaarik /'kɑːrɪk/	Kratus /'kreɪtuːs/
Lostris /lɒs'trɪs/	Memnon /'memnɒn/
Nephthys /'nefθɪs/	Osiris /əʊ'saɪərɪs/
Pharaoh Mamose /ˌfeərəʊ mɑː'mɒhsi:/	
Qebehsenuef /ˌkeb'senu:ef/	
Quebui /'kebwi:/	Rasfer /'ræsfə/
Seth /set/	Taita /ta'ɪtɑː/
Tanus /'tænu:s/	Thebes /θi:bz/

6

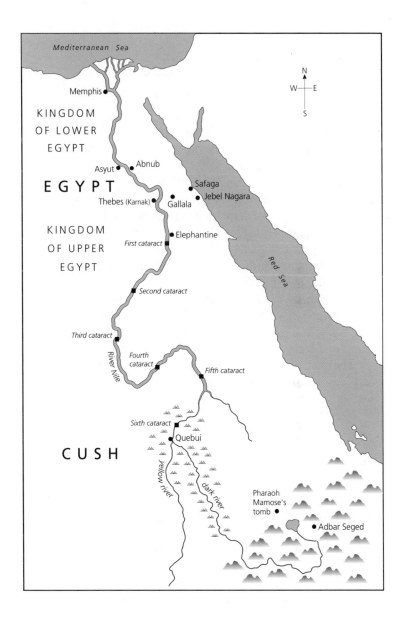

The Places in This Story

1

Taita the Slave

On 5th January 1988, Dr Duraid Al Simma – an expert on Egyptian history – found an Ancient Egyptian tomb[4] on the west bank of the River Nile. In the tomb there were ten large jars which were filled with papyrus scrolls.

These records were almost 4000 years old. They had been written by an Egyptian slave, and they told the story of his life.

The slave had lived at a time when Egypt was divided into two kingdoms and was ruled by two pharaohs. One of these pharaohs ruled the northern part of Egypt – the land known as Lower Egypt. The other pharaoh ruled in the south. The southern land was called Upper Egypt.

The Pharaoh of Lower Egypt had his capital city at Memphis. The Pharaoh of Upper Egypt lived at Elephantine, but his land was controlled by a governor. The Governor lived in the twin cities[5] of Thebes and Karnak.

The man who wrote the documents which were found in 1988 had been a slave in the Governor's palace at Thebes. His name was Taita.

Here begins the story of Taita the Slave.

———

I am Taita the Slave. My story begins in the heart of Egypt. My life has been long and I remember many things. But this story begins on the day that I remember best. I remember that day more than all the other days of my long life.

The River Nile flows through the land of Egypt and it flows through my story. On the day when my story begins I was thirty years old. That day, the Nile was shining as brightly as metal under the desert sun.

I was sitting in a long boat – a galley. The boat was moving quickly over the water. Many men rowed the boat and many

8

boats followed behind us. All these boats were galleys of the Egyptian navy. The men who rowed the galleys were soldiers of Pharaoh Mamose, King of Egypt.

When we moved close to the river bank, we saw people from the villages. They were working in the fields beside the Nile and they were lifting water from the river for their crops[6]. They used long poles with leather buckets hanging from their ends. These were called *shadoofs*. As I watched, the shadoofs dropped and lifted, dropped and lifted, like the oars of our boats.

Our boat glided by the papyrus that grew all along the banks of the river. The papyrus reeds were tall and thick. Often, they hid our view of the fields and the villagers.

I was sitting at the back of the boat and looking straight ahead. In front of me, two lines of powerful rowers pulled at the huge wooden oars. I looked down between the men to the front of the boat.

A young woman – she was only fifteen years old – sat in the bow[7] of the boat. Her name was Lostris and she was very beautiful. And that day, she was also very happy. She was happy because we were going to hunt hippopotamuses[8]. She had never come with us on a hippopotamus hunt before. She was singing with happiness.

'Taita,' she called to me. 'Taita, sing with me.'

So I began to sing with her. Many people have told me that I have a beautiful voice. Lostris and I sang perfectly together.

I will always remember her on that day. She was so young, so beautiful, and so full of life. As the boat moved swiftly, the river flashed with light and the two of us sang like beautiful birds. I wanted to sing to make her happy. I wanted to make her happy because I loved her as if she was my daughter. But I was not her father, I was her father's slave.

Yes, I am Taita the Slave. I am not a free man. I was sold

Our boat glided by the papyrus that grew all along the banks of the river.

into slavery when I was a child, and I grew up as a slave in the land of Egypt. And on that day, long ago, I was the slave of Lostris's father, Lord Intef, the Governor of Upper Egypt.

Our King, the Pharaoh Mamose, was the ruler of Upper Egypt, but Lord Intef governed the land for him. Lord Intef was the most powerful man in Upper Egypt, and he was a cruel man. Lostris was his only child and it was my job to protect her. I looked after her and I amused her. I tried to do what she wanted me to do. But I had to obey her father.

I remember how Lostris and I sang on the boat that day and I remember how we laughed. But although I laughed and I smiled, I felt afraid! I felt afraid because Lostris's father did not know that she was in the boat with us. Lord Intef did not want Lostris to hunt hippopotamuses – but I had disobeyed him.

Lord Intef did not let his daughter go anywhere alone. We lived in the Governor's Palace at Thebes. Lostris was allowed to walk around the palace and she could walk along the banks of the Nile. She could even go out into the city – as long as there were guards around her. But Lostris was never allowed to be alone.

I went everywhere with her, and the guards came too. We could never get away from the guards. The guards watched over Lostris, and they watched over me as well. They watched everything we did and they listened to everything we said. Then they made a daily report to Lord Intef.

Neither of us was free. I was a slave, but Lostris was a prisoner! Yes, although she was the Governor's daughter, she felt like a prisoner. To her, the palace was like a great prison with high walls. Lostris was young – she wanted to be free. She wanted to go out without the guards. And she wanted to see a hippopotamus hunt on the river.

'Oh, Taita, please, please, *please* let's go to the hunt,' she often said.

11

'No, it's impossible,' I always replied. 'Your father will not allow it. What will he say if we go without asking him? He will be very angry. He will kill me!'

But again and again Lostris said, 'Please, Taita, let's go to the hunt. You'll look after me – I'll be safe with you. I *do* want to see the hippopotamus hunt.'

At last I had agreed. But I felt afraid, because we had not told her father, Lord Intef, what we were going to do.

I tried not to worry. Lostris and I were singing beautifully together. Then we heard another voice. It was the deep voice of Tanus, the commander of the galley. Tanus was a fine young man, and he was my friend. But when Lostris turned and smiled at Tanus, I felt even more afraid. I felt more afraid because I saw at once that they liked each other very much. They looked into each other's eyes.

Most Egyptians have dark hair and dark eyes. Lostris herself had beautiful dark eyes. But Tanus was unusual – he had fair hair and blue eyes. His mother had been a foreign slave.

Before I go on with my story, I must tell you more about Tanus. He was a soldier, but he was not an *ordinary* soldier.

Ten years before, when Lostris and Tanus were children, the Governor of Egypt had been a man called Lord Harrab. Harrab had governed the *whole* of Egypt for Pharaoh Mamose. He was a good and wise Governor, but he was a simple man. He did not really understand people. He trusted 'friends' who were really enemies. One of these 'friends' was Lord Intef.

Great trouble had come to Egypt while Lord Harrab was Governor. The Pharaoh's brother had led a rebellion[9] and he took half the kingdom for himself. That was when the land was divided. After the rebellion, the Pharaoh's brother ruled Lower Egypt and Pharaoh Mamose ruled Upper Egypt.

At the same time, there was much violence in the land.

Bands[10] of thieves and murderers controlled the country-side. People were not safe in their villages. Merchants[11] and travellers were often killed on the roads.

The Governor, Lord Harrab, tried to destroy these bands of thieves, but he failed in this task. Lord Intef and his friends spoke to our Pharaoh.

'All the troubles of Upper Egypt are caused by Lord Harrab,' they said. 'He is a weak man. Our land needs a strong Governor. Only a strong man can destroy the thieves and the false Pharaoh in Memphis.'

Pharaoh Mamose listened to these words. He believed Lord Intef and his friends, so Pharaoh made Lord Intef the Governor of Upper Egypt and he took all of Lord Harrab's land and property away from him. Soon after that, Lord Harrab died. Many people believed that Lord Intef had killed him.

What is the connection between Lord Harrab and Tanus? It is this – Lord Harrab was the *father* of Tanus.

The boy Tanus grew up without a mother or a father. He joined the Pharaoh's army when he was very young. For some years, no one knew that the young soldier was the son of Lord Harrab – not even Tanus himself. But he found out about this later – and so did Lord Intef!

Tanus was strong and clever. He became the youngest captain in the Pharaoh's army. Pharaoh Mamose was pleased with him. At the age of twenty, Tanus became Commander of the group of soldiers called the Blue Crocodile Guard[12]. The Guard travelled in galleys on the Nile. That is why Tanus was leading the hippopotamus hunt that day.

2

The Hippopotamus Hunt

Now I must go on with my story about Lostris, Tanus and myself. The three of us were in the galley on the River Nile, that day of the hippopotamus hunt. I was the protector of Lostris and I was the friend of Tanus. But I was also the slave of Lord Intef, who did not want his daughter to leave the palace. And Lord Intef certainly did not want his daughter to meet the son of the previous Governor.

We moved on under the hot sun. Then suddenly, a lookout[13] shouted, 'There's a hippopotamus ahead of us!'

A moment later, I saw a huge grey hippopotamus swimming in the water in front of the boat. It was moving away from us.

'Row harder!' Tanus shouted to his men. He moved to the front of the boat. He picked up a great bow[14] and he prepared to fire an arrow at the hippopotamus. I had made the bow for Tanus. It had a name – Lanata. It was a powerful bow and it fired heavy arrows. Only a man as strong as Tanus could pull the string of that bow.

But not even Tanus could kill a hippopotamus with arrows. We had to get close to the animal so that the soldiers could kill it with spears.

'Mistress! Mistress![15]', I called to Lostris. 'Come to the stern of the boat. You will be safe here with me and Commander Tanus.'

But, as usual, Lostris would not listen to me.

'This is exciting!' she called out. 'I want to see the hippopotamus.'

Soon more hippopotamuses appeared. We had found a herd of them. The other boats had been rowing behind us, but now they spread out around the animals and the hunt began. Arrows flew through the air. Spears flashed in the sun. And soon, there was blood in the water.

'We will kill the biggest one!' Tanus shouted. He fired an arrow, and then another. Both his arrows hit the largest hippopotamus, and the animal dived below the surface of the water. Our galley raced towards the place where the hippopotamus had dived. The rowers pulled hard at the oars and the boat moved swiftly into the deep water in the middle of the river. But we could not see the hippopotamus.

Then suddenly, the animal surfaced[16] right in front of us. It was a huge male hippopotamus. When it surfaced, it almost overturned the boat. The front of the galley was thrown up into the air, and so was Lostris.

'My little one!' I shouted. I saw the open mouth of the hippopotamus. The animal's teeth were like white knives. I saw Lostris fall from the boat. She landed on the animal's back. Tanus's two arrows were deep in the creature's[17] neck and she held on to these.

Tanus threw down his bow and picked up a sword. Then he jumped onto the back of the hippopotamus. With both hands he thrust[18] the sword into the animal's neck. There was a fountain of blood. The creature stopped moving for a moment, then it dived under the surface of the water again.

'All swimmers go to the bow!' I shouted. 'We must save Lostris and Tanus!'

All the soldiers who could swim dived over the side of the boat. I am a strong swimmer and I dived into the river too. The water was dark with blood and I could see nothing under the surface. I was terrified.

Then Tanus and Lostris surfaced near me. They were laughing. I was glad that they were safe, but I was very angry.

'What will your father say about this?' I said to my mistress.

Tanus and Lostris laughed as the soldiers helped them to climb back into the galley. I sat apart from them and dried

15

*Tanus and Lostris laughed as the soldiers helped them to climb
back into the galley.*

myself in the sun. I was still angry and I did not speak.

After a while, Lostris came to me and kissed me.

'The soldiers told me that you commanded the boat when we were in the river,' she said. 'They said that you ordered the soldiers to save us. And you got wet. You are very brave, Taita!' She smiled her sweetest smile. My anger immediately vanished – it always did when Lostris smiled.

The dead hippopotamus rose to the surface of the water. Some of the soldiers tied ropes to it and the rowers rowed the boat to the river bank. Other galleys joined us there and they brought many more dead hippopotamuses with them. The hunt had been a great success.

Soon, the villagers left their fields and came to the river bank. We cut the skins off the animals, then cut up the meat into large pieces. We gave some of it to the villagers and they started to cook it.

It was the time of the festival of the god Osiris[19]. To celebrate this festival, the village people always rested from their work for four days. Now we had brought them a feast of hippopotamus meat. They ate it hungrily and they drank beer made from corn.

There was plenty of meat, but there were also many people. The villagers tore at the pieces of meat as if they had not eaten for days. They tore at the meat and they cut it with knives. They were not very careful – I saw a man cut off one of his own fingers. Soon, the villagers were fighting over the meat. The corn beer was very strong, and they were getting drunk.

I had to make sure that a share of the meat went to the Governor's palace, so I told the soldiers to collect some of it. I watched them press great pieces of the red meat into big wooden barrels.

The sun was setting when I started to look for Lostris. Where was she? I felt afraid again. I ran along the river bank calling, 'Lostris! Lostris! Where are you?' But I could not find her, and I could not see Tanus either. I hoped that they were not alone together.

Quickly, I found a soldier called Kratus. Kratus was a close friend of Tanus.

'Where are they?' I asked him. 'Tanus and Lostris – what are they doing?'

He pointed towards the Temple of Hapi[20], the river god. 'They're over there,' he replied.

I ran quickly towards the temple without stopping to thank him.

Tanus and Lostris were inside the temple. They were kneeling close together and they were talking quietly.

'Taita! I'm glad that you have come,' Lostris said as soon as she saw me. 'Listen, I have news. I want to marry Tanus!'

She looked so happy.

'Oh, no,' I said. 'Oh, no, no!' I loved Lostris and I hated to spoil her happiness. But I felt very afraid.

'Your father —,' I began.

'You will speak to Lord Intef for me, won't you, my friend?' said Tanus. He got up and put his arm around my shoulder. 'Lord Intef will listen to you – you're his adviser.'

'Yes, my father always asks Taita for advice,' Lostris said happily. 'Taita will arrange everything. He always knows what to do.' She laughed.

I said nothing. They were so young and they were so much in love. They did not understand that a Governor of Egypt's daughter could not marry a soldier from the army.

Suddenly Lostris looked at my face and she stopped laughing.

'Why are you so sad, Taita?' she asked quietly.

'Your father will kill me,' I replied.

3

Pharaoh Mamose Arrives

The boats returned to Thebes the next morning. I sat with Tanus and Lostris. They were happy, but I was sad and I was very worried. I tried not to show my sadness.

We had carried the hippopotamus meat aboard the boats – barrels and barrels of meat, smoked and salted[21]. It was meat for the Festival of Osiris.

I usually enjoyed the festival, but that year I was not expecting a happy time. Lord Intef would be waiting for me at Thebes, and I had a lot to explain to him.

Lord Intef lived in the Governor's Palace at Thebes. Pharaoh Mamose, the ruler of Upper Egypt, did not live in Thebes – he lived in a Palace at Elephantine. But every second year, Pharaoh came to our city for the Festival of Osiris. He came for the great celebration which took place in the Temple at Karnak, on the edge of the city. So when our boats reached Thebes, my master, Lord Intef, was preparing to welcome Pharaoh the next day. But he had not forgotten about *me*.

Tanus and Lostris said goodbye to one another on the palace wharf[22]. I wanted Lostris to go back to her room in the palace as quickly as possible. Tanus had another job to do straight away. His boat was going to travel south. I was glad about that – I did not want him to be in the palace when I told Lord Intef about Lostris's plans.

When I took Lostris into the palace, she kept looking back at Tanus.

Let me tell you something – Lord Intef did not really care about his daughter as a person. He did not care about her because he did not love her. But he cared about who she would marry. He wanted her to marry someone rich and powerful. Although Lord Intef was already the richest man in Upper Egypt, he wanted more gold, more land, and more power. He hoped to get these from his daughter's husband.

———

I found Lord Intef in the palace garden. He was about to eat a meal. Slaves were putting dishes of food on a low table in front of him. The only other person with him was Rasfer, the Commander of the Palace Guards.

Lord Intef had strange, yellow eyes. I often thought that he looked like a big cat. He was a very dangerous man and, although I was his favourite slave, I was afraid of him.

Lord Intef ordered the slaves to leave the garden. Then he pointed at me and at the food.

I approached the low table. As usual, I took a small piece of food from each dish. Lord Intef watched my face carefully. He never ate food which someone else had not tasted first. He was afraid that someone would try to poison him.

The food was very good. I smiled. The food was safe, so Lord Intef smiled too. He was a very handsome man when he smiled. He began to eat and I stood and waited. Rasfer, the Commander of the Palace Guards, watched me. He was an ugly, cruel man. He carried a long whip in his hand. I was afraid of Lord Intef, but I was afraid of Rasfer too.

'Tell me about the hippopotamus hunt, Taita,' Lord Intef said quietly, when he had finished eating.

I told him about the hunt. I told him how much meat we had brought for the festival. He seemed pleased.

'Now, Taita, tell me why my daughter went on this hunt with men from the Blue Crocodile Guard. I did not give my permission.' Suddenly I felt cold, but Lord Intef continued to smile as I replied.

'You were busy, my lord,' I said. 'I did not want to worry you. I took good care of your daughter.'

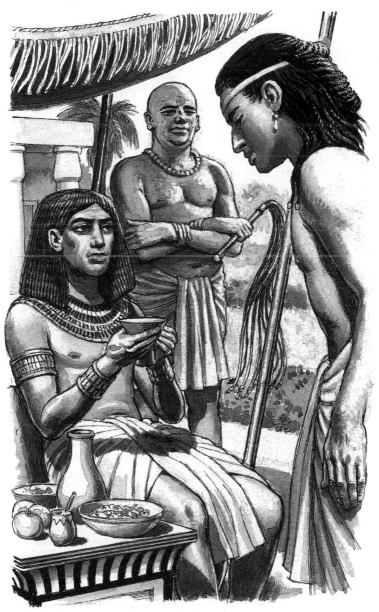

I was afraid of Lord Intef, but I was afraid of Rasfer too.

'You know that my spies tell me everything,' Lord Intef said quietly. 'I am not pleased with you, Taita, but I will give you a chance to explain what happened.'

I fell to my knees[23] in front of Lord Intef. 'My lord,' I said, 'your daughter is fifteen years old. She is a woman now and she wishes to have a husband.'

Lord Intef put his foot on my neck and pressed my face to the floor. 'Does she?' he said angrily. 'Daughters do not decide to marry, Taita. Fathers make decisions for them. And slaves do not disobey their masters.' He called to the Guard Commander. 'Rasfer! This man is valuable to me. Do not kill him. But remind him that he is a slave and that I am his master!'

Rasfer used his whip. I could not see it, but I heard it before he hit me on the back. I screamed as the whip lashed my skin.

'Ten lashes will be enough,' said Lord Intef. 'My daughter is still innocent[24]. The priests of the Temple of Isis[25] have already questioned her.'

———

Afterwards, a slave boy cleaned my wounds. I was lying on my bed when Lostris sent for me. I walked slowly to her room. I felt terrible.

She rushed up to me as soon as I reached her room.

'They're sending him away! They're sending him away!' she screamed and she beat her small hands against my chest.

'Who? Where?' I asked. My mind was not clear because I was in pain.

'Tanus. They're sending Tanus to the south. I'll never see him again! I'll die if they send him away!' She started to cry.

I tried to comfort her. I knew where Tanus had gone.

'Tanus has only gone to Elephantine,' I told her. 'He will escort[26] Pharaoh Mamose here to Thebes for the festival. You will see him again soon, I promise you that.'

'But those priests – those terrible priests! They asked me so many questions about Tanus. And they told me never to see him again.'

I held Lostris in my arms for a long time. At last she dried her tears and looked up at me. Suddenly she seemed older. I saw strength and determination in her face. 'I shall speak about this to Pharaoh,' she said. Then she fell asleep in my arms and I put her into her bed.

For a few minutes, I watched her as she slept. I had cared for Lostris every day since she was a baby. Now she looked like a small child again.

But I did not stay with her for long – I needed sleep myself. My master expected Pharaoh to arrive before midday the next day, and he needed my help in the morning.

———

The next day, a great crowd of people waited on the wharfs of Thebes. They looked at the boats that came from the south.

Pharaoh Mamose came down the river from Elephantine. He sat in a huge, heavy barge[27]. Two hundred rowers rowed the barge towards the wharfs and the Blue Crocodile Guard rowed their boats around it. Tanus was in the bow of the leading boat, which was called the *Eye of Horus*[28]. Tanus was a tall, strong man and his fair hair shone in the sun as he directed the other boats towards the wharfs.

Lord Intef stood on the palace wharf and Lostris stood beside him. She was watching Tanus. I stood with them, but I was watching Pharaoh. He sat on a golden throne[29] in his barge. His face was covered with white make-up[30]. He looked neither young nor old. In fact, he was more than sixty years old. On his head he wore the double crown of Egypt – the white crown of Upper Egypt joined to the red crown of the Delta[31]. But everyone knew that a false Pharaoh – the red Pharaoh of the Delta – ruled the lower part of Egypt. That Pharaoh ruled the land almost as far south as Thebes itself.

23

Although he came to Thebes for the festivals, our own Pharaoh stayed in Elephantine most of the time. He felt safe there. His kingdom stretched from Thebes to the First Cataract of the Nile, near Elephantine. Pharaoh Mamose never went far from the river. He controlled everything and everyone on the Nile within the borders of his land. He had a strong navy. But he was growing old and weak, and he did not control the countryside *beyond* the river. That land was controlled by thieves and murderers, and Pharaoh did not have the power to destroy them. Mamose was not one of the Great Pharaohs. The Great Pharaohs – the rulers who built the huge pyramids at Giza – lived a thousand years ago. Those days of greatness are now only a memory.

As we watched, Pharaoh Mamose's barge turned towards the wharf. It was a heavy boat and the strong current[32] was flowing behind it. As the royal barge began to turn towards the wharf, the steersman lost control of the boat. The barge turned right round. Now its stern was moving towards the stone wharf and it was going to be smashed!

But the leading boat of the Blue Crocodile Guards had also turned. A tall man with golden hair threw a rope to the royal barge. It was Tanus.

'Tanus!' Lostris shouted.

Then the great crowd of people started shouting too – 'Tanus! Tanus! Tanus!'

The men on the royal barge tied Tanus's rope to the bow of their boat. Then Tanus's crew pulled at the oars of the *Eye of Horus*. They tried to pull the royal barge safely away from the wharf.

Tanus's boat could not stop the royal barge without help. The barge was too heavy. But suddenly a strong wind began to blow from the north. We had always called the north wind 'the wind of the god Horus'. But afterwards, we called it 'Tanus's wind – the breath of Horus'.

24

The wind helped Tanus's boat to move the royal barge to safety. The barge stopped for a moment. Then it turned slowly and moved steadily towards the wharf behind the *Eye of Horus*. Soon the barge was tied to the wharf.

The guards lifted Pharaoh's throne and carried him from the barge onto the wharf. All the people fell to their knees as Pharaoh passed them.

I, too, fell to my knees. Ordinary people were not allowed to look into the face of Pharaoh. But, before I bowed my head[33], I saw Pharaoh look carefully at the crowd. He looked at Lord Intef and he looked at Lostris. He did not look at Tanus.

———

The most important part of the Festival of Osiris was the play at the Great Temple of Karnak. There is always a play at the Festival of Osiris. The play tells how the great god Ammon-Ra had two children, Osiris and Seth. It tells how one of these gods was good and the other bad.

That year, I had written the play and the music myself. And I had supervised[34] the building of a stage in the temple, where the play was going to be performed.

The day before the performance, I met Tanus near the Great Temple. I was glad to see him because he had an important part[35] in the play. I wanted to talk to him about the play, but he wanted news of Lostris. He expected to see Lostris after the festival. I knew that he would not be allowed to see her, but I did not tell him that. I did not want to make him unhappy.

'Have you learnt all your words, Tanus?' I asked him.

Tanus nodded and smiled. 'Yes. I'm ready,' he replied.

25

4

The Festival of Osiris

The next day, late in the afternoon, Pharaoh came to the Temple of Osiris at Karnak. All the people of Thebes were there to watch the play. Pharaoh's face was painted white. He wore magnificent clothes and jewels. On his fingers were many rings. He sat on a throne and he looked at my stage.

The masons[36] who had built my stage had made a large water container next to it. During the play, water was going to run from this container into a channel with reeds next to it. The water represented the River Nile.

The play of Osiris began. It was in three acts.

In the first act, the god Osiris walked by the River Nile alone. Suddenly, his brother Seth came up behind him, carrying a big knife. The part of Seth was played by Rasfer, the Commander of the Palace Guards. He was an evil-looking man and he was perfect for the part. Seth attacked Osiris and pretended to cut his body into fourteen pieces. The crowd screamed and the priests cried out. Osiris was dead!

We had started the play late in the afternoon because we wanted darkness in the temple for the second act of the play. As darkness fell, the soldiers who stood at the back of the stage lit torches[37].

Lostris came onto the stage. She played the part of the goddess Isis. Another woman, who played the part of the sister of Isis, Nephthys, followed Lostris onto the stage. Isis and her sister were looking for the body of Osiris.

I had made a statue out of wood and clay and I had cut it into fourteen pieces. This statue was to be the body of Osiris. After a few moments, Isis found the body of Osiris and joined the pieces together again.

'Osiris is in the underworld now,' Lostris said to the crowd. 'But soon I will have his child – I will give him a son.'

Lostris's face was very beautiful in the light of the torches. As she said those words, Pharaoh leaned forward and stared at her. I noticed his interest, and so did Lord Intef.

Perhaps Pharaoh thought that those words – 'I will give him a son' – were spoken directly to *him*. Pharaoh Mamose had no son of his own.

Next, Lostris, in the part of the goddess Isis, went to the back of the stage. When she came forward again, she held a tiny baby in her arms. She showed the baby to the people.

'Here is the new-born son of Osiris,' she said. 'Here is the Lord Horus, god of the wind and the sky.'

The second act of the play ended. I walked onto the stage and spoke to the people in the temple. I spoke to them about Horus's life as a boy and about how he grew into a man.

'He became tall and strong,' I told them. 'He wanted revenge for the murder of his father.'

In the third act, Tanus came onto the stage. He was playing the part of the god Horus.

The crowd recognized the fair-haired commander. They cheered, and even Pharaoh smiled.

Next, Rasfer, playing the part of the god Seth, came onto the stage. He looked ugly and evil, even though he wasn't wearing make-up.

'Who are you looking for?' Seth asked.

'I am looking for the murderer of my father,' Horus replied.

'Then look no further,' Rasfer said. 'I am Seth, the eater of stars and the destroyer of worlds. I killed Osiris!'

I had made wooden swords for these two actors. Now they lifted their swords and began to fight. But suddenly I realized that something was wrong. Rasfer was no longer acting. I saw the hate in his eyes and I also saw that his sword was not made of wood. He had changed the wooden sword for a sharp metal one – a real sword!

'Tanus,' I shouted, 'he is trying to kill you!'

Tanus turned his head to see who had called to him. At that moment, Rasfer jumped forward to attack Tanus. He pointed his sword at Tanus's face.

For a moment, I stopped breathing – I was very frightened. But Tanus was lucky that day. My masons had not done their work well. Water from the container had flowed out of the channel and onto the stage. As Rasfer attacked Tanus, his feet slipped in the water. He tried to push his sword into Tanus's eye, but he only cut Tanus's forehead.

Blood ran down Tanus's face and fell onto the stage. There was blood in Tanus's eyes and, for a moment, he could not see. He fell to his knees. Rasfer raised his sword again. He was going to stab Tanus in the neck. But Tanus grabbed Rasfer's legs and threw him backwards. There was a terrible sound as Rasfer's head hit one of rocks I had placed on the stage beside my 'river'. Rasfer lay still on the floor of the stage. I hoped that he was dead, but he was only badly wounded.

Soldiers from the Palace Guards ran onto the stage and carried their commander away. And at the same time, Tanus walked to the front of the stage. He wiped the blood from his face and spoke directly to Pharaoh.

'I am Horus,' he said in a loud voice. 'Hear me!'

Pharaoh Mamose nodded his head. The crowd became silent. Tanus looked like an angry god. At that moment, many people believed that my friend was the god Horus – I'm sure of that.

'Our land of Egypt is divided,' Tanus said. 'We are surrounded by enemies. The countryside is controlled by murderers and thieves – the men who are called Shrikes. Our Pharaoh is surrounded by dishonest men too – even the royal palace is full of thieves!'

'Tanus,' I shouted, 'he is trying to kill you!'

The crowd was astonished. No man could speak to Pharaoh like this and expect to go on living. But perhaps it was not a man who was speaking – perhaps it *was* a god.

'These thieves are the followers of Seth,' Tanus continued. 'Destroy them now, as I destroyed Seth himself. The Shrikes are enemies of our land and of our people. Hear me, Pharaoh. Save your people!'

Pharaoh Mamose was angry. He was a king. He did not allow anyone to tell *him* what to do! He did not want to hear any more from this man who was dressed as a god.

Pharaoh stood up and walked away. Everyone fell to their knees as Pharaoh left the temple.

'Isn't Tanus wonderful?' Lostris whispered to me.

I said nothing. I had seen the anger in Pharaoh's face. And so had Lord Intef, who was smiling cruelly. Tanus was a dead man[38] – I was sure of that.

The soldiers of Pharaoh's Royal Guard came for Tanus in the night. They came to the camp of the Blue Crocodile Guard. Tanus stood in the middle of the camp. His men stood all around him.

'We will fight with you, Tanus,' said his friend Kratus.

'There will be no fighting,' said Tanus. 'I will obey Pharaoh.'

The soldiers took him to the palace. They brought him to Pharaoh and Lord Intef.

'Tanus, son of Harrab, you have spoken against Pharaoh,' said Lord Intef.

'I have only spoken the truth,' said Tanus. 'Our land *is* divided and controlled by thieves.'

Pharaoh spoke.

'Then *you* shall destroy these thieves. I will give you men and weapons. And I will give you two years to complete this task. You will have until the next Festival of Osiris to rid[39]

30

Egypt of these thieves in the countryside. You will have two years to do this. If you fail, you will die.'

Lord Intef smiled. He thought that it was an impossible task. Also, he had something else to announce – something that would make Tanus very unhappy.

'Pharaoh is kind and generous,' said Lord Intef. 'He is happy today because he is going to marry a new wife. And *I* am happy because he has chosen my daughter, Lostris. Lostris will be the new wife of our Pharaoh.'

A few minutes later, Tanus left the palace and returned to his camp. He looked unhappy but he did not speak to anyone.

5

A Gift From Lord Intef

The next morning, the whole city knew that Pharaoh had ordered Tanus to destroy the Shrikes. And everyone thought that it was an impossible task. The Shrikes were too strong and they lived in the desert, far from the river. An army could not find them and destroy them.

But I will write more about this later. First, I must tell you about the marriage of Pharaoh and Lostris.

When I went to Lostris on the morning after the play, my young mistress was very unhappy. No one had asked her if she wanted to marry Pharaoh Mamose. But the wish of the Pharaoh had to be obeyed. Lostris was only fifteen years old and Pharaoh Mamose was nearly fifty years older than she was. But Pharaoh wanted a son. Although he had married many wives, he had never had any sons.

31

'He is an old man,' said Lostris sadly. 'I want to marry Tanus. I do not want to marry an old man.'

'It is the wish of Pharaoh,' I said. I was sad too, but I could not stop the marriage, and neither could Lostris.

Soon the priests from the Temple of Isis came for Lostris. The Palace Guards came with them. They took my mistress to the temple to prepare her for her marriage. These preparations would take several days and I could not follow her to the temple.

————

My mistress wore a simple red dress for her wedding. It was the colour of wine. And it was the colour of the red silt[40] which is carried down the River Nile every year and which brings life to Egypt. In our land, people think that red is a happy colour. But that day Lostris did not look happy. Her face was pale and her eyes were sad. She looked as if she wanted to be somewhere else – somewhere far away. She was doing what she had been ordered to do. But she did not want to do it.

Pharaoh wore his double crown and a false beard. He wore many jewels and gold rings. He held the flail and the crook[41] of the Kings of Egypt in his hands. A hundred slaves carried him on his golden throne to the Temple of Isis. All the people fell to their knees as Pharaoh passed.

Lord Intef wore a heavy gold chain around his neck and gold bracelets on his arms. I stood next to my master. He had already asked my advice about a marriage gift for Pharaoh. I had suggested five thousand gold rings and a hundred squares[42] of land.

The Chief Priest of Osiris blessed the marriage. Then Pharaoh broke a loaf of bread in half, ate some of it, and drank from a cup of wine. Next, he handed the bread and wine to Lostris. She ate and drank, but she said nothing until Lord Intef asked her a question.

'What gift do you want from me, my daughter?'

Lostris answered, 'I want only one thing, my father. Give me the slave Taita.'

Lord Intef tried to smile, but he was angry. I was his slave, but I was his adviser too. He had told me many secrets. He did not want me to leave his palace, because he was afraid that I would tell Pharaoh his secrets.

'A single slave is a small gift for the wife of Pharaoh,' Lord Intef said. 'Take a hundred squares of land.'

But Lostris repeated, 'Give me the slave Taita.'

Pharaoh Mamose moved his crook and flail very slightly – this was a sign that he agreed with Lostris's request. I bowed my head. Neither I nor Lord Intef could refuse to obey the wish of Pharaoh. But before I went to stand beside my mistress at the left hand of Pharaoh, Lord Intef whispered angrily to me, 'Taita, you are a dead man!'

A few hours later, I left the palace of Lord Intef. I was no longer his slave, I was now the slave of Lostris. I walked behind Pharaoh Mamose and his new wife to the wharf where the royal barge was waiting. Soon we were sailing up the river towards Elephantine.

Had I escaped the cruelty of Lord Intef at last? I had been his slave since I was a boy. Now he hated me – I knew that. He hated me because I knew so many of his secrets. I hoped that I would be safe in the Royal Palace at Elephantine.

Elephantine is an island. It is close to the First Cataract on the Nile, near the southern border of Egypt. The Royal Palace covers much of the island, and a city spreads over the rest of it, down to the banks of the river. Only the city of Thebes, and the city of Memphis in Lower Egypt, are larger than Elephantine.

For the first few months at the palace, my mistress was sad all the time. But after that, she began to feel happier. She was

33

Lord Intef whispered angrily to me, 'Taita, you are a dead man!'

still very young and Pharaoh Mamose was kind to her. He treated her like a daughter and Lostris began to think of him as a new father. The ladies of the palace were kind to her too, and they were also kind to me. They often sent gifts to my mistress, and sometimes they sent me gifts too.

Lostris was no longer unhappy, but she did not forget Tanus.

'Tanus is young,' I said to her, 'and Pharaoh is old. You will marry again when he dies.'

I could not forget Tanus either. We did not hear from him and I often asked myself, 'What is Tanus doing? How will he and his men destroy the Shrikes?'

One morning, I received a short message from Tanus's friend Kratus. 'Tanus has disappeared,' the message said.

I wanted to tell my mistress about this, but I wanted to get more news before I spoke to her. Tanus had disappeared, but how? And where? I did not know, and the messenger from Thebes could not tell me.

————

The next day, I found a large basket in the centre of my room. The room smelt of fresh mangoes and pomegranates, which are my favourite fruits. I was pleased that someone had sent me a gift. I took off the lid of the basket and put my hand in, to take the largest, ripest mango. Suddenly, a hissing sound made me jump back and a terrible black head appeared from under the fruit in the basket. It was the head of a giant hooded cobra[43], and it hissed and spat at me!

The black snake came out of the basket and slithered across the floor. The snake lay between me and the doorway. I stayed very still – I was afraid to move.

Then I heard Lostris call, 'Taita, where are you?' A moment later, she was standing in the doorway. She saw the great black snake and she stood still too.

Now the snake turned towards Lostris. It was going to

strike at her. I still had the mango in my hand and I threw
the mango at the snake. I was lucky – the fruit hit the snake
on the head.

Lostris was very brave. As the cobra's head fell forward,
she jumped onto it. Quickly, I pulled a knife from my robe
and stabbed the snake's body, behind the head. It wrapped its
long body tightly around my legs, but I stabbed again and
again until the cobra stopped moving.

'I know where this horrible thing came from,' Lostris said
angrily.

'Yes, it was a gift from your father,' I said. 'He has not forgotten me and I am not safe here.'

After that, I showed Lostris the message from Thebes. 'I
am sure that Tanus is safe,' said Lostris. 'But there is a secret
in this message. Tanus needs you. You must go to him, Taita.'

I could not leave Pharaoh's palace without his permission, and
I did not think that I would get it. So Lostris and I made a plan.

The next day, before sunrise, I went fishing alone. I took
a bag of clothes with me and I rowed from the island to the
opposite shore of the river. There I put on my disguise[44] – the
clothes of a priest. Then I overturned my small boat and
pushed it away from the shore.

There are many crocodiles near Elephantine. They are
always hungry. So when someone found my overturned boat
in the river, everybody thought that I had been eaten by a
crocodile. Only Lostris knew that I was not dead.

Quickly, I travelled north, away from Elephantine. I saw
many real priests on the road, and many other travellers too.
People travelled in large groups – caravans – because everyone was afraid of the Shrikes who controlled the countryside.

I did not walk all the way to Thebes. Half a day's journey
from Elephantine, there is a wharf. From there, I travelled by
boat down the river.

———

When I reached Thebes the next evening, I kept my head covered. Many people in the city would recognize the face of Taita the Slave, and I did not want Lord Intef to find me.

I visited the tavern[45] where the men of the Blue Crocodile Guard often went to drink. There I found Kratus, the friend of Tanus.

'What do you want, priest?' Kratus asked me when I approached him. My disguise was good!

'Where is Tanus?' I asked him quietly.

He looked at me carefully. 'Taita!' he said, after a moment.

'Don't shout my name,' I said. 'Can we talk secretly?'

He nodded and took me to a quiet room.

'I haven't seen Tanus since the day after Pharaoh left the city,' he told me. 'Before he left, Tanus gave me the command of the Blue Crocodile Guard.'

I was shocked – this was not good news!

'But where has he gone?' I asked.

'He said that he was going to the other side of the river. He said that he needed some time for thinking. He was drunk when he left.'

Suddenly, I understood. 'I know where he is now,' I said. 'It is a place that only he and I know about. I will go to him there tomorrow.'

6

Tanus Is Found

The next morning, I crossed the river in a small boat. It was still the season of the flood. At that time of year, the Nile was full and the fields near the river were covered with water. There are many irrigation channels[46] in which the water runs through the fields of crops. The channels end in swamps[47], far from the river. I followed a road beside one of these irrigation channels and I travelled towards the east.

The road and the channel ran between low hills. Travelling alone here was dangerous, because thieves watched the road from these hills. But I was wearing the clothes of a poor priest, so I thought that I would be safe. Priests have no gold – they are not worth robbing!

I walked for half a day. The hot sun burned down on my face. I saw no one until I was almost at the place where I expected to find my friend. Then, for a moment, I thought that I saw Tanus on the road.

A man was coming towards me. I saw that he had unusual fair hair, like Tanus's hair. The man was leading a donkey and a woman was riding on the animal.

'How far is it to Thebes?' called the man.

'It's half a day's walk from here,' I said. 'But why are you on the road alone? There are many thieves in the hills.'

'My wife is going to have a baby,' the man replied. 'We are going to her family in Thebes. The baby will be born very soon. We cannot wait to join a caravan of other travellers.'

'I wish you a safe journey,' I said. Then I left the hills behind me and walked into the wide, flat swampland.

There is a small single hill in the middle of the swampland. Tanus and I found it one day, when we were hunting. The path through the swamp is narrow and dirty. Few men ever go there. But Tanus had built a hut on that hill, and he sometimes stayed there when he wanted to be alone.

As I had expected, I found Tanus in the hut. He was asleep. Empty wine jars lay on the floor. I knew that he had been drinking too much wine.

'Tanus!' I shouted. 'It's almost midday and you're still lying in bed!'

Tanus jumped up and picked up his sword. 'What? Who is it?' he shouted. 'A priest? No – it's Taita!'

He walked forward unsteadily.

'My Lady Lostris would not be proud to see you,' I said. 'You are drunk. You look like a dirty animal. Have you forgotten who you are? Have you forgotten the Lady Lostris? Have you forgotten your duty to Pharaoh Mamose?'

Tanus looked ashamed[48], but he replied angrily.

'They have forgotten *me*!' he shouted 'I have lost everything. I cannot marry the woman that I love – she is married to another man. I do not want to live any longer. Leave me here.'

'Very well,' I said. I was thinking quickly. I had to make Tanus come back to Thebes with me. There was only one thing that I could do.

'Very well,' I continued. 'I will not give you the message from Lostris. I will go.' Then I turned and walked away.

'Wait, Taita, please wait!' Tanus called.

But I did not wait. I walked through the swamp back towards the road. Then I stopped. I heard a sound behind me. Tanus was following me through the swamp. He was carrying a bag and a sword. My plan had succeeded.

'Where are you going?' he asked.

'I'm going back to Thebes,' I said, 'and you are coming with me.'

We reached the road and we started walking towards the Nile.

'What is the message from the Lady Lostris?' he asked.

'She loves you and she cares for you,' I replied.

'But she is the wife of Pharaoh,' said my friend.

'Yes – but not for ever,' I said.

We had not gone far when we saw two bodies lying in the road ahead of us. As we got closer, I recognized the body of the traveller with fair hair, and the body of his wife. They had been killed only a short time before. The man's face was covered with blood.

'Shrikes,' said Tanus. 'The Shrikes did this.'

'Yes, Shrikes killed them and stole their donkey,' I said. 'Remember your promise to Pharaoh, Tanus. You promised to destroy the Shrikes.'

'I can see five of them now,' said Tanus quietly. 'Look over there.'

A path led towards the west from the road, into the desert. It led towards the low hills. In the distance, five men were leading a donkey along the path.

Tanus began to run and I followed him. We were both swift and silent, and the Shrikes did not hear us or see us. Soon, Tanus – who was in front of me – ran up behind the last man in the group. With one stroke, he cut off the man's head with his sword.

For a moment, I was shocked. I knew that Tanus was a sol-dier, but I had never seen him kill a man. He killed another of the thieves before the rest of the Shrikes could turn. The dead men had carried short spears. I picked up one of them while Tanus fought the three remaining men.

One of the Shrikes tried to get behind Tanus. I stabbed him with the spear. He screamed, and Tanus turned and killed him. Another Shrike ran straight at Tanus, and my friend killed him too. The last man, the one who had been leading the donkey, ran away. But I followed him, holding my spear out in front of me. The man turned to fight me, but I

40

The Shrikes did not hear us or see us.

thrust the spear into his body. He fell down. He was dead – I had killed him.

'Well done, Taita!' said Tanus. 'You have surprised me.'

I had surprised myself – I dislike violence. But these men were thieves and murderers.

———

We left the bodies of the five thieves in the desert and we led the donkey back to the road. We looked again at the bodies of the murdered man and woman.

'Look at that man's fair hair, Tanus,' I said. 'It's very unusual. It looks like your own hair.'

Suddenly I had an idea. 'Put his body on the donkey,' I said. 'I'll take the body back to Thebes and I'll say that it is your body. I'll say that Tanus is dead.'

'It's a good idea, Taita, but Lostris must not believe it,' Tanus replied.

'I will send a message to Lostris. Now, you must put black mud in your hair, so that nobody will recognize you. Meet me at the camp of Kratus tonight.'

I explained my plan as we walked towards Thebes. We separated before we reached the river and I went on alone to the camp of Kratus. I took the dead man's body to the camp of the Blue Crocodile Guard.

'I have found Tanus, and he is well,' I told Kratus. 'Tell your men. But I want everyone else to believe that he is dead.' I pointed to the dead man on the donkey. 'I want them to believe that this is Tanus's body.'

Kratus made arrangements to bury the fair-haired man's body. He knew that everyone would soon hear the news. He was certain that Lord Intef's spies were all around him. 'Tanus is dead,' he said sadly to everyone he met. I'm sure that the spies took the news to the Governor's Palace that same day.

That night, the men of the Blue Crocodile Guard met together. They waited for Tanus to appear. When he came,

42

his face and hair were covered with mud, but the men knew him immediately. They were happy to see him again.

'Bring my bow, Lanata, to me,' he said. 'I have a plan to destroy the Shrikes. I want to leave Thebes in the morning and I want to move quickly. I need ten men to come with me. We will travel to the coast of the Red Sea. The rest of you can follow us more slowly. We will meet at Jebel Nagara in seven days' time.'

7

The Shrikes Attack!

We left Thebes before dawn the next day. Tanus led ten of his men and I went with them. We marched towards the east all day and stopped only for short rests. Soon, I was exhausted[49].

On the road, we passed two large groups of travellers, but we did not join these caravans. Although it was safer to travel in a large group, a caravan moved slowly. And Tanus wanted to reach the coast as soon as possible. So we moved quickly, and we reached Jebel Nagara in four days.

Jebel Nagara is a small fishing village on the coast of the Red Sea. I had been there before, on business for Lord Intef. The countryside around the village was controlled by the Shrikes. They always watched the roads for caravans coming along the coast. We wanted more information about the Shrikes, but we could not get any news in Jebel Nagara.

While Tanus waited in the village for Kratus to arrive with the other men, I travelled on a fishing boat up the coast to Safaga. Safaga is a much larger port – most of the trade of Upper Egypt passes through Safaga. The Shrikes always watched the roads which led to it.

I went to Safaga because I knew a merchant there. When I arrived at the port, I went to his house. A slave stood at his garden gate.

'Tell Tiamat, your master, that the healer[50] who saved his leg is here,' I said to the slave.

Some years before, I had helped Tiamat the merchant after he was attacked by Shrikes. He had been terribly wounded in one of his legs. If I had not helped him, he would not have been able to walk again.

I waited while the slave went into the house. A few minutes later, Tiamat walked slowly into the garden. He came to the gate and he looked at me carefully. I was still wearing the robes of a priest, but after a moment, he recognized me.

'Taita! My old friend!' he said. 'What can I do for you?'

We talked in the garden. 'I want information about the Shrikes,' I told him.

'I hate the Shrikes,' said Tiamat. 'I will tell you everything I know about them. They rob us of more and more every year. I will help you destroy them.'

_____

After we had talked, Tiamat sent me back to Jebel Nagara in one of his own ships. The ship carried cargo[51] for Tanus and his men. It was a very strange cargo!

When I reach Jebel Nagara, Kratus and the other men had arrived from Thebes. They looked at my cargo in surprise. 'Do you really want us to wear these?' Kratus asked. He held up some black robes. They were women's clothes!

'Yes, Kratus,' I replied. 'I want the Shrikes to try to capture you and your soldiers. Shrikes will not attack a hundred armed men, but they *will* try to capture a caravan of slave women!'

The men thought that this was a great joke. They laughed noisily. Tanus told them to put on the women's clothes and to keep quiet. He did not want anyone to hear their voices.

Soon, most of the soldiers were dressed as women. The robes, which covered them from head to foot, were hot and uncomfortable to wear. I know this, because I was wearing a woman's robe too. Tanus was dressed as a rich merchant, and ten of his men wore the uniforms of guards. They were going to lead the 'female slaves' through the desert.

We all went aboard Tiamet's ship and sailed back to Safaga. When we arrived in Safaga, Tanus bought donkeys, food, and water containers for our caravan.

'The desert road is dangerous,' said one of the merchants. 'Don't you know about the Shrikes?'

'I have ten guards,' answered Tanus. 'I am not afraid of thieves.'

The merchants of Safaga laughed when they heard this. 'He is a dead man,' they said to each other. 'The Shrikes will kill him and his guards and they'll steal his money and his slaves.'

But when our guards loaded the donkeys, they hid many weapons in the baggage which the animals carried.

The next day, the caravan moved out of Safaga along the desert road. Tanus had ordered his men not to speak until we were far from the town.

A caravan moves slowly. We knew that it would take us more than a week to reach Thebes. We made a camp in the hills that night.

———

The men were not comfortable. They disliked wearing women's clothes and they were complaining loudly when we set off the next morning. But Tanus ordered them to be silent.

After a few hours travelling, we saw three men. They stood in the road in front of our caravan and held up their hands to stop us.

45

'Greetings, travellers, what can I do for you?' Tanus called to them.

One man came forward. He was an evil-looking man with one eye.

'You must ask what *we* can do for *you*!' said the man. 'Have you heard of the Shrikes?'

'Yes, I've heard of those wicked thieves,' said Tanus. 'But who are you?'

'I am Shufti, Baron[52] of the Shrikes. I have killed many, many men – so many that I cannot count them all. Give me twenty of your slave women and I will let you pass.'

Tanus did not answer. He walked up to Shufti and suddenly grabbed the man's arm. He twisted the arm up behind the thief's back. The other two Shrikes prepared to attack him, but Kratus and his guards quickly grabbed them.

'I am Kaarik the merchant,' said Tanus. 'I go where *I* want to go. *Nobody* takes anything from me. You will remember my name.'

Tanus pulled a whip out from under his cloak. The guards held the three thieves down on the ground. Tanus beat them with his whip until they cried out in pain. Then the guards let the thieves go.

'You will suffer for this,' said Shufti angrily. 'I will bring every Shrike in Egypt to kill you. We will find you wherever you are. You cannot hide from us!'

This was exactly what Tanus wanted to hear. He wanted as many Shrikes as possible to come after us.

'Good,' he replied. 'Bring your friends. We will beat them as we have beaten you!'

Our caravan moved on. But now we were not thinking about getting to Thebes. We were looking for a place where we could defend ourselves against an attack by a large number of Shrikes.

———

46

'You must ask what we can do for you!' said the man.
'Have you heard of the Shrikes?'

The ruined town of Gallala stands halfway between Safaga and Thebes. That is where we went next.

At one time, Gallala had been a large oasis[53], but now most of the water had dried up. Because of this, everybody had left the town. All the houses were empty.

There was an old, broken temple which stood on a small hill at one end of the town. It was a good place for defence. Fresh water from a spring ran into a container at the back of the temple. Many wild animals came there to drink.

We camped in the temple and Tanus prepared our defences.

'We will be ready for the Shrikes when they come,' he said.

We waited for two days. While we waited, we rested. Then, at dawn on the third day, a loud voice called to us from the desert, and Tanus went outside.

'Kaarik the merchant, are you awake?' the voice called. 'I am Shufti, Baron of the Shrikes. I have come to take everything from you. And I have come to take your head from your body!'

'Then come here and take it!' Tanus shouted back.

In the early morning light, I saw Shufti raise his hand. About a thousand men stood up. Slowly, they advanced on[54] the ruined temple.

'Shufti has been busy,' said Tanus. 'Good! But there are more Shrikes than I expected.'

Tanus's guards moved quickly into position at the back of the temple. They took out their bows. Tanus carried his own great bow – the bow called Lanata.

The men who were dressed as women stayed near the side walls of the temple. They pretended to be afraid as the first of the Shrikes ran into the building.

The entrance to the temple was narrow. Only two or three men could come through the doorway together. They were an easy target[55] for the arrows of the guards.

The first Shrikes were killed by Tanus's arrows – he could shoot very quickly. Ten men went down, but more and more Shrikes ran into the temple. They ran over the dead bodies. Tanus and the guards took out their swords.

At that moment, Shufti entered the temple.

'Capture the merchant alive!' the baron called to his men. 'I want him to die slowly.'

Nearly one hundred men pressed into the narrow temple. They circled around Tanus and the men who had been fighting with him. Suddenly, Tanus called out. This was a signal for the rest of us. We threw off our women's clothes and attacked the Shrikes, from the sides and from behind. It was a massacre[56]! Our men killed several hundred Shrikes before the rest tried to run away. But there was no escape for them – they were trapped in the temple!

I saw Shufti, Baron of the Shrikes, trying to climb over the temple wall. I threw a piece of stone at him, and he fell down. I ran over to him and I held my knife to his throat. Suddenly, he recognized me as Lord Intef's slave. My master in Thebes had done business with him in the past.

'Taita, let me go,' Shufti said. 'I will reward you well. Lord Intef will reward you too.' But I wanted nothing from him or from Lord Intef. Shufti was our prisoner. And soon, the rest of his men were either killed or captured.

The Shrikes' camp was not far away. Tanus sent me with fifty men to collect their baggage. There were only a few guards at the thieves' camp, because most of the Shrikes in the area had come to Gallala. We took about one hundred and fifty donkeys. The animals were loaded with treasure from raids on merchants' caravans. I led the donkeys back to Gallala, where Tanus was waiting.

Tanus looked so handsome that day. His golden hair shone in the sunlight and he looked like a god. For the first time, I heard his new name. After that battle, his men called him 'Akh-Horus' – the brother of the god Horus.

Only a few dozen Shrikes were alive after the battle. Tanus went to talk to the prisoners.

'I will give you a chance to live,' Tanus told them. 'But you must tell me the names of the leaders of all the bands of Shrikes. Tell me their names, and tell me the places where they camp. If you do this, I will not kill you.'

Most of the prisoners refused to speak. Their heads were cut off. We also killed the men who were badly wounded.

One prisoner, a young boy, fell to his knees in front of Tanus. 'Akh-Horus,' he said, 'I am Hui, of the band of Basti the Cruel. I was forced to become a Shrike. But I will be your servant now.'

Tanus made Hui a member of the Blue Crocodile Guard. We learnt a lot from him. We learnt the name of the leader of all the Shrikes. This man called himself Akh-Seth – the brother of the dark god Seth.

Shufti, Baron of the Shrikes, would not tell us anything, but we did not kill him. He was a valuable prisoner. We took him back to Safaga and left him there. Tiamat the merchant promised to keep him in a prison.

Some of our soldiers had been killed. The survivors[57] no longer dressed as women. They wore the uniforms of the Blue Crocodile Guard and the merchants of Safaga welcomed them to the town. 'You have done a great thing,' they said. 'Please go on with your task. Save the land of Egypt from the Shrikes.'

'I will find the other Shrikes and I will destroy them,' Tanus told the people of Safaga. Then he spoke quietly to me.

'Taita,' he said. 'Please return to Elephantine. Start your journey today. Go to Lady Lostris and tell her that I am alive and well.'

50

8

The Royal Hunt

My journey back to Elephantine took many days. When I arrived there, I went immediately to the Royal Palace. I was wearing the robes of a priest, so no one recognized me. I went to the room of Lady Lostris. One of her slave girls sat by the door.

'What do you want, priest?' the girl said. 'My mistress is sick. You cannot see her.'

'She will see me,' I said.

Then the girl recognized me. She jumped to her feet.

'Taita! But you're dead! You're a ghost!' she said.

Then she ran into the slaves' quarters[58]. As she ran she shouted that the ghost of Taita had come for the Lady Lostris.

I went into Lostris's room. My mistress was almost a ghost herself. She lay on her bed. She was terribly thin and pale and I saw that she was starving[59]. Her lips were moving. 'He is dead,' she whispered.

I knelt by the bed and I looked into her eyes. I smiled at her.

'My Lady,' I said. 'I have a message for you.'

'Taita, is that you?' she whispered. 'Tanus is dead, and I will join him soon in the Afterlife.'

Before the Blue Crocodile Guard travelled to Jebel Nagara, I had sent Lostris a message about Tanus. But now I realized that she had not received the message. She thought that Tanus was dead.

'When did you last eat?' I asked her.

'I shall never eat again,' Lostris answered weakly. 'I shall go where Tanus has gone.'

'Tanus is alive and well and he will come to you,' I told her.

51

'I shall go where Tanus has gone,' Lostris answered weakly.

'Do not lie to me,' she said. 'He was buried in Thebes. Everybody says so.'

'*I* do not say so. *I* say that Tanus is alive,' I replied. 'I saw him a week ago. He commands the Blue Crocodile Guard and he is destroying the Shrikes for Pharaoh Mamose. When he has finished his task, he will come to you.'

Lostris looked at my face, and at last she believed me.

'He mustn't see me like this,' she said. 'Bring me some food.'

I brought her some milk and honey. It was difficult for her to eat at first. I fed her like a baby.

Then a messenger arrived from Pharaoh. The messenger's name was Aton and I knew him well. He looked at me carefully.

'Taita, we thought that you were dead. Pharaoh has heard about your return. He wants to see you immediately.'

I went with Aton to the royal apartments. Pharaoh Mamose spoke to me in his private room.

He also looked at me carefully. Everyone believed that I was a ghost. Suddenly, I realized that Pharaoh was afraid of me! And then I had an idea.

'Great Pharaoh,' I said, and I fell to my knees in front of him. 'The god Anubis[60], Lord of the Dead, has sent me here. He has sent me to you from the Afterlife. My task is to protect the Lady Lostris. She has been very sick, but with my help she will soon recover.'

'Yes, yes,' said Pharaoh quickly. 'You must protect her. Do not leave her again until she is well. Now go!'

I went quickly. Pharaoh believed that I had returned from the dead – I wanted him to go on believing that. Now my task was to make Lostris well.

———

My mistress recovered quickly. She was young and, when she began to eat normally, she soon became strong.

53

'How do I look, Taita?' she asked me, after a few days. 'Is my face ugly? Am I getting fat? When will Tanus come? You will bring him soon, won't you?'

Every day I told her that she looked better. 'And Tanus will come soon, when you are completely well,' I told her.

As time passed, we often had news about Tanus, and it was good news. The battle against the Shrikes was going well. Another stronghold[61] of the thieves had been captured by Tanus and his men, and then another.

At last, a time came when merchants could travel safely to the coast again. The people of Upper Egypt could travel on the roads in safety. And Tanus had another name. Now he was 'Akh-Horus, the Destroyer of Shrikes'.

———

It was the time of the flood once more. Every year, the water in the Nile rises and floods the fields of Egypt. Elephantine was near the First Cataract on the Nile, and from the island we could see the white water rushing over the cataract. The river rose, and every day the priests of the temples measured the rising water.

'The crops will grow well this year – there will be a good harvest,' the priests told Pharaoh.

The people were glad at this news. They built new irrigation channels. They planted new crops in the fields furthest from the river. For years they had not planted crops in these fields. 'Why plant crops there when thieves take everything?' they had always said. But now the danger from the Shrikes was over.

One day, I received a message from Hui – the Shrike who had joined the Blue Crocodile Guard. Hui had shown Tanus the strongholds of many of the Shrike bands, and Tanus had promoted[62] him. He was now a good friend to Tanus.

'Lord Tanus greets you,' Hui wrote in his message. 'He is

still searching for Akh-Seth, the Lord of the Shrikes. But he is nearby now. He is watching. He will come to you soon.'

I told Lostris about the message. She was excited by the news. After that, she waited and watched every day.

———

Lostris was now strong enough to go out. Pharaoh led a great hunt on the west bank of the river to celebrate her recovery. The whole court[63] went out to hunt gazelles[64], and Lostris came with us. Hundreds of people spread out across the desert to the west of Elephantine.

The hunt lasted for a whole day. I looked after Lostris. We rode slowly on two donkeys at the back of the hunting party.

During the afternoon, the wind grew very strong. I saw a storm coming out of the desert. 'Mistress,' I said. 'We must find shelter[65] from this storm.'

Lostris agreed with me and we rode back towards the Nile. Near the bank of the river there was a group of old tombs. Thieves had taken everything from them years ago and now they were like empty caves.

The wind was blowing more and more violently and the air was full of sand. Soon we could hardly see. I pulled Lostris towards the tombs. 'We must shelter there,' I said. 'We cannot find our way in this storm.'

At that moment, a strange figure appeared out of the storm. It was a black shape moving towards us. For a moment, I thought that it had wings! It came out of the cloud of sand that blew around us.

But then I saw that the strange figure was a man dressed in a cloak. The wind was blowing the cloak away from his body so that it looked like a pair of wings.

Lostris cried out. But she did not cry out in fear.

'Tanus!' she shouted. She ran into his arms and they held each other for a long time.

Then Tanus spoke to me. The wind was so strong that I

55

could hardly hear his words, but he pointed to the tombs.

'We must shelter Taita, old friend,' he said. 'But do not leave me alone with the wife of Pharaoh. I am full of love for her and I fear what will happen if we are alone together.'

But, for the only time in my life, I did not listen to my friend. I led our donkeys towards the tombs. The animals carried our tents and our food and water. I led them into the largest tomb and Tanus and Lostris followed me. Then I left my friend and my mistress with the animals and I ran to another tomb. It was the furthest tomb from the one where I had left the young lovers. There I hid from the wind and the sand.

The hours passed. Darkness fell. Somehow I slept, though I had no food or water.

_____

When I awoke, the wind was not so strong, and outside I saw the first light of day. I went to the largest tomb to look for Lostris.

I had to dig away a little sand to get into the tomb. My mistress was asleep inside. She was sleeping peacefully on mats made from papyrus reeds. The donkeys stood in the corner of the tomb, but there was no sign of Tanus.

Soon, the other hunters found us. They had been searching the desert, calling the name of Lady Lostris. I shouted to them. They took us to Pharaoh, who was not far away.

'You have saved the life of the Lady Lostris,' Pharaoh said. He put a gold chain round my neck. This was a fine reward.

'Thank you for saving me, Taita,' Lostris said. But I knew that she was really thanking me for leaving her alone with Tanus the night before.

_____

A month passed, and then it was the time of the Festival of Osiris again. It was now two years since Pharaoh had given

Tanus the task of destroying the Shrikes. We made preparations to go to Thebes.

On the day before the start of the festival, the whole court travelled down the river on many boats. Lostris and I travelled on Pharaoh's royal barge. We were alone together in the stern of the barge.

Lostris spoke to me very quietly. 'Taita, my friend, I have something to tell you.' She paused for a moment. 'I am going to have a child.'

'Are you sure?' I asked.

'Yes, I am sure,' Lostris said. And she added, 'It is the child of Tanus.'

I had to think quickly! What was I going to tell Pharaoh? Lostris had told me that Mamose had never tried to give her a child. He had treated her like a daughter and he had never made love[66] to her. The news of a baby would be a surprise to him.

Fortunately, I was able to make use of my 'special powers' from the gods. Pharaoh still believed that I had been sent back from the Afterlife by the god Anubis. As a result, he was still a little afraid of me.

Later that day, I went to talk to him. I fell to my knees in front of him.

'Last night I had a dream, Great Lord of Egypt,' I told Pharaoh. 'The goddess Isis came to me in my dream. She told me that the Lady Lostris will have the child of the god Horus. It is a sign that tonight the Lady Lostris will receive the child of Pharaoh.'

Pharaoh smiled. 'A child! A son, at last,' he said. He was happy. 'I have waited so long for a son. It *will* be a son. It *must* be a son. There must be another Pharaoh of my family after I have gone to my tomb. Send the Lady Lostris to me tonight.'

We had been very lucky – Pharaoh had believed my story!

And there was some truth in my words. I had said that Lostris would have the child of Horus, and Tanus was now called Akh-Horus. I hoped that the child would be a boy.

9

The Truth About Akh-Seth

We arrived at Thebes – the beautiful City of a Hundred Gates – for the Festival of Osiris. A great crowd of people was waiting for us on the wharfs.

Lord Intef, Governor of Upper Egypt and the father of Lostris, stood at the front of the crowd on the palace wharf. Beside him stood Rasfer, Commander of the Palace Guards. Both those men hated me – I knew that. I stayed close to Pharaoh and the Lady Lostris.

The next day, we went to the temple at Karnak and watched the Play of Osiris. It was not so interesting this year. I had not written any of it. Neither Tanus nor Lostris had parts in it. And the god Horus did not speak to Pharaoh at the end of the play!

———

The Kings of Egypt have always built great tombs in the valley which lies across the river from Thebes – the Valley of the Kings. On the day after the play, Pharaoh Mamose wished to visit his own tomb. He wanted Lostris to go with him. We crossed the Nile and travelled along the wide road that leads to these tombs.

The tomb of Pharaoh Mamose was cut into the rock of the valley. Everything was already prepared for his death. There was a huge gold sarcophagus[67] to hold his body. There were canopic jars[68] to hold his internal organs.

Artists had painted the walls of the stone rooms of the tomb. The pictures showed scenes from The Book of the Dead[69]. Priests of Anubis were ready to embalm Pharaoh's body with expensive oils as soon as he died. Then they would wrap it in mummy cloths[70], and place it in the wooden coffin which would fit inside the gold sarcophagus.

Everything was wonderful. The tomb was filled with treasure – there were huge piles of gold and jewels. We thought that there had never been so much treasure in one place at one time. Pharaoh was very pleased. We returned happily to Thebes.

_____

The next day, the Festival ended with a great meeting of the people of Thebes in the Temple of Osiris.

Pharaoh sat on a tall throne. He wore the double crown of Egypt on his head and he held the crook and flail in his hands. His chief advisers stood near him. The Lady Lostris sat at his right hand, and Lord Intef stood at his left. Thousands of people knelt in the great square of the temple. They waited for their King to speak.

Suddenly, we heard the sound of a trumpet and the bronze doors at the back of the temple opened. A man with golden hair walked through the doors. He looked like a god.

'Akh-Horus!' a woman screamed.

Then all the people shouted, 'Akh-Horus!'

It was Tanus. He led six prisoners behind him. Their hands were tied together with ropes. He approached the throne of Pharaoh and spoke.

'Great Lord of Egypt, you ordered me to destroy the Shrikes. I led a thousand men into the desert and attacked the secret strongholds of these thieves and murderers. Their power is now destroyed. I have brought their leaders here for you. Now, only one remains free – the Lord of the Shrikes.'

'Speak, Tanus,' answered Pharaoh. 'Tell me the name of

this man who is Lord of the Shrikes.'

'He calls himself Akh-Seth,' said Tanus. 'And he is here today, in this temple. Let the prisoners point to him.'

The people were very quiet and still. They wanted to hear the name of the Lord of the Shrikes.

One of the prisoners was Shufti, Baron of the Shrikes, who had been captured at Gallala. Slowly Shufti lifted his hands and pointed to Lord Intef.

'That is the Lord of the Shrikes,' he said.

Then the other prisoners pointed at Intef too.

'What do you say to this, Lord Intef?' Pharaoh asked.

'This man is a liar,' Intef replied. 'There is no truth in his words. Does he have any proof?'

'Does he have any proof?' Pharaoh asked Tanus. 'Can you prove that the Governor of Upper Egypt is Lord of the Shrikes?'

Tanus was silent. I could see that he did not have proof.

'My Lord. I can prove it!' I shouted out. 'I was the slave of Lord Intef. I know the secret places where he hid his treasure – the treasure of the Shrikes.'

Lord Intef looked at me with anger and hatred. 'A slave must not speak against his master,' he said. He moved his hand. Rasfer pulled out a knife and ran towards me. He was going to kill me in front of Pharaoh, but Tanus stepped forward. He knocked Rasfer down and took the knife from him.

Pharaoh Mamose pointed at Rasfer and Intef. 'These men are now prisoners,' he said to his guards. Then he looked at me. 'I want to see your proof, Taita,' he said quietly.

I led Pharaoh and his advisers to the palace of Lord Intef. I showed them a secret door in the Governor's private rooms. 'The treasure is in an underground room,' I said. 'But the room is sealed. We need masons to break open the walls.'

Masons came and removed stones from the wall. Soon, they had found the secret room. There were fifty-three boxes

'Akh-Seth is here today, in this temple. Let the prisoners point to him.'

of gold and twenty-three boxes of silver inside the room. There were also boxes of jewels. Everybody could see that Intef was a very rich man – richer than Pharaoh Mamose. Pharaoh was very angry at this. *He* wanted to be the richest man in Egypt.

'We will take this treasure,' ordered Pharaoh. 'Intef and all the Shrikes must die. Fix their hands and feet to the gates of Thebes with nails. Leave their bodies for the birds to eat!'

———

The next day, seven men were nailed to the gates of Thebes and left to die in the sun. Tanus's six prisoners and Rasfer, the Commander of the Palace Guards died that day, but Lord Intef had escaped in the night. He had poisoned his guards and he had disappeared.

I guessed that Intef had gone to the false Pharaoh in Memphis – but I was wrong, as I will soon tell you.

Our own Pharaoh, Mamose, rewarded Tanus and me. He gave me two boxes of gold. But because I was a slave, the gold became the property of my mistress, Lostris. It was a great amount of money and Pharaoh liked to keep money in his own family!

Tanus was given his father's title – Lord Harrab – and all his father's property was given back to him. Pharaoh ordered Tanus to build five fleets[71] of war galleys with Intef's treasure. Now the Shrikes were destroyed, Pharaoh Mamose's soldiers were strong enough to attack the army of the false Pharaoh in Memphis.

———

Pharaoh Mamose's court stayed in Thebes after the Festival of Osiris. Lostris tried to meet Tanus whenever he came to the palace. But they could never be left alone together. I often carried messages between them. Pharaoh never suspected[72] that the father of Lostris's unborn child was Tanus.

Lostris used my gold to build hospitals and schools in

Thebes. The people of Thebes loved her for this.

'I love Thebes,' she said to me one day. 'I want to stay here forever. I don't want to go back to Elephantine.'

One day, she even spoke to Pharaoh about this in front of the whole court.

'My Lord, I was born in Thebes,' she said. 'I want your son to be born in Thebes too, not in Elephantine.'

I was astonished. Lostris was asking Pharaoh to move the court to Thebes. It was something that would change the lives of thousands of people.

Pharaoh was astonished too – his face told me that! But Lostris was seventeen years old now, and she was Pharaoh's favourite wife. He could not say no to her. He thought for a moment and stroked his false beard. Then he spoke.

'Very well, the court will move to Thebes,' he said. 'Taita, you must design a new palace on the west bank of the river. I have decided to call my son Memnon – Ruler of the Dawn. We will look eastwards at the rising sun every morning, from the new palace.'

Soon after this, the army started to prepare to attack the false Pharaoh of the Delta. As the months passed, Tanus was promoted again. He was given a new title – Great Lion of Egypt. He commanded the army and navy in the whole of the northern part of Upper Egypt.

At this time too, we started work on the Palace of Memnon. I supervised the masons. I did not have a moment's rest. Everybody else was happy, but I had no time to be happy or sad!

10

The Battle at Abnub

It was the middle of the night when Lostris's son was born. I was afraid that the child might have golden hair, like his real father. But fortunately, the baby's hair was black, like his mother's.

Pharaoh ordered a great celebration for the birth of Memnon. All the people of Thebes gathered in the Temple of Osiris at Karnak. Pharaoh raised the child in his arms.

'This is my son, Memnon, Prince of Egypt,' he said. 'From this time on, his mother shall be second only to Pharaoh. She is now Lostris, Queen of Egypt.'

Queen Lostris was pleased, but she wanted more.

'Prince Memnon must have a tutor,' she said. 'And the Prince must have a guardian, to care for him if his father dies while he is still a child. My slave, Taita, will be the boy's tutor. And I wish Tanus, Lord Harrab, Great Lion of Egypt, to be his guardian.'

Pharaoh was pleased to agree to these requests. And he was even more pleased when Tanus won a great victory at Asyut the following year.

In the battle, our army and navy took the town of Asyut from the false Pharaoh of Memphis. Pharaoh Mamose ordered another celebration. After that, Tanus came to the palace often. He was the man who was going to be the guardian of Prince Memnon, so he had a reason to be alone with Lostris. They were happy.

The happiness of Lostris and Tanus lasted for five years. Then one day, one of our galleys came to Thebes with news from the north.

The false Pharaoh of Memphis was dead and his army

was destroyed. That was good news. But the reason why it had happened was *not* good. A new enemy had come to Egypt.

'We call these enemy warriors[73] *Hyksos*,' said the messenger from the galley. 'They are terrible. They have weapons of hard metal and they sail across the desert in ships. They move as fast as the wind and they destroy everything in their path!'

When he heard this news, Pharaoh Mamose called his War Council[74]. The council ordered Tanus to move north with half of the army and navy. 'The other half will follow soon,' said Pharaoh. 'You must defend the border between Upper and Lower Egypt. You must keep the town of Asyut!'

Pharaoh sailed down the river with some ships of his navy. He wanted to see these Hyksos warriors for himself.

'How can these people *sail* across the desert?' he asked. 'It's impossible!'

The whole court travelled with him. We camped at a village called Abnub on the east bank of the Nile. Queen Lostris and Prince Memnon were there too.

Tanus commanded thirty thousand men on land and another five thousand on the river. He sent galleys towards Memphis to gather news. The galleys returned in four days. The captains of the galleys told us terrible things.

'We saw towns and villages on fire,' they said. 'We saw clouds of dust. The clouds are moving south. The Hyksos are coming this way.'

Soon, we too saw a great cloud of dust approaching from the north. Our war trumpets sounded and our men got ready for the attack.

Soldiers with heavy spears were in the front ranks[75] of our army. They stood with their shields together. The points of their spears rested on the ground in front of them. Behind these men stood the archers, soldiers who fought with bows and arrows. And behind the archers stood soldiers with swords which were made of bronze.

Pharaoh sat in his golden throne on higher ground. From there he could look down on our army, and I stood beside his throne.

We looked at the cloud of dust as it came closer. We saw black figures moving in the cloud. They came towards us very swiftly. Then they stopped and the dust began to disappear.

I saw many new things that day. I saw strange animals which looked like donkeys. But they were larger, stronger, and swifter than donkeys. I saw horses for the first time!

These horses pulled small carts. Afterwards we called these carts 'chariots', but we had no name for them that day. At first we did not understand what we were seeing. Then we realized that it was in these chariots that the Hyksos 'sailed' across the desert.

For more than a thousand years, Egyptians had pulled carts across the desert using wooden rollers. These Hyksos chariots did not move on rollers, they moved on wheels. We saw wheels for the first time that day. Why had no Egyptian thought of wheels? It was such a simple idea!

Soon, there were more surprises for us. The King of the Hyksos rode forward in his chariot. His beard was black and curled. He carried a bow, but it was not like the bows of the Egyptians. We had simple wooden bows that curved only when we fastened the strings to their ends. The bow of the Hyksos king had been made with a curve *before* the string was fastened to it.

Tanus picked up his own bow, Lanata. Tanus was very strong and he could shoot an arrow further than any other Egyptian. He shot an arrow at the Hyksos king. The Hyksos king lifted the shield on his left arm and the arrow struck it. Then he used his own bow. He shot an arrow higher and further than any Egyptian could shoot. His arrow flew over the heads of our soldiers and landed at the feet of Pharaoh himself. At that moment, I knew that we were going to lose the battle.

The first lines of Hyksos chariots started to move. They gathered speed[76], but they did not come directly towards our front ranks. Instead, they moved along the flanks[77] of our lines of soldiers.

The chariots had long curved knives on the hub[78] of each wheel. These spinning knives cut the legs of the soldiers at the ends of our lines. Soon our soldiers were running to get out of the way of the chariots.

The first Hyksos chariots found a weak point in our ranks and crashed through it. More chariots followed them. Our men were cut down by the chariot knives. The chariots ran through our lines to the rear. Then they turned and the enemy attacked our men from all sides.

The Hyksos archers fired thousands of arrows at us. Our archers shot back at them, but our arrows could not reach the Hyksos. Our bows were not as powerful as theirs.

The Hyksos archers aimed at our captains, who wore helmets with coloured feathers on them. Soon they had killed all the captains. Now our soldiers had no one to give them orders and they were very frightened. Our soldiers turned and ran – they ran in all directions. A great cloud of dust rose up from the ground. No one could see what was happening. But still the Hyksos soldiers advanced. They killed everyone in their path. It was a massacre.

I stood by the golden throne of Pharaoh. He sat looking in horror at the dust and the confusion. Everyone could see him, above the dust of the battle. Suddenly he stood up, and as he stood, an arrow struck him in the chest. He gasped and fell back onto his throne.

A moment later, Tanus and Kratus were at his side. They

An arrow struck Pharaoh in the chest.

lifted him up and laid him on a shield.

'Come to me, the Blue Crocodiles!' shouted Tanus. 'Form the tortoise[79]. Move back to the ships.'

The men of the Blue Crocodile Guard 'formed a tortoise' around Pharaoh. We moved as quickly as possible towards the river. Our archers were still shooting arrows at the Hyksos army. They quickly learned to shoot at the horses rather than at the men in the chariots.

The Hyksos chariots chased us to the swamps near the river. The chariots could not cross the soft, wet ground and we reached our ships safely. But we were the only Egyptians who were safe. Behind us, thousands of our soldiers were being killed.

When the women on the royal barge saw that Pharaoh was badly wounded, they began to wail[80]. We laid Pharaoh on the deck of the barge and Lostris held his hand. The king was dying and he spoke weakly.

'Lostris is Queen of Egypt. She will rule the land until my son, Memnon, is old enough to be King.'

'I will do as you command,' said Lostris.

'There is one more thing,' said Pharaoh. 'When I am dead, you must seal my tomb and keep it safe.'

I looked at Lostris. At this moment, nothing was safe from the Hyksos – we knew that.

'I will do as you ask,' said Lostris.

———

Tanus went back to the battlefield, and he led the remaining soldiers to the Nile. There were not enough men left to sail all the ships. We had to burn half of our fleet.

Half our soldiers had died in the battle. But although the Hyksos were better fighters than our men on land, they had no ships. We sailed towards Thebes and the Hyksos could not follow us.

Pharaoh Mamose died soon after the sun set that evening.

There was nothing I could do to save him. Behind us, on the river bank, the town of Asyut was burning.

The royal barge moved slowly against the current. The Hyksos, moving along the river bank, passed us in the night and captured some of our ships. Early the next morning, we saw them. They were using the ships to move their horses and men from the east bank of the Nile to the west bank. We caught them by surprise. Now, we Egyptians were in a stronger position for battle.

'The Hyksos do not know how to sail ships,' said Tanus. 'We must attack them at once. Sail towards the bank!'

Soon we were close enough to one of the river banks to see some of the Hyksos clearly.

'Look over there,' I said, and I pointed to a man who was wearing Egyptian clothes. 'There is a traitor. He's showing the Hyksos how to sail the ships. I know that man. It is Lord Intef!'

'I will kill him!' said Tanus.

11

Escape from Egypt

The Hyksos were not good sailors. We crashed our boats into some of the boats that they had captured, and they quickly sank. Our archers shot hundreds of flaming arrows into the other Hyksos ships.

Tanus tried to sail closer to the east bank. He wanted to kill Intef and so did I. But we were beaten back by the arrows of the Hyksos archers. Still, we had won a small victory – only a few of the Hyksos had succeeded in crossing the river. And now we could win another victory – we could win some knowledge!

We easily captured the few men, and the horses and chariots, which the Hyksos *had* landed on the west bank.

'We must find out all we can about horses and chariots,' I told Tanus. 'Then we will be able to breed[81] our own horses and build our own chariots. One day, we will be able to fight against the Hyksos with their own weapons.'

Tanus shook his head. He pointed to the horses. 'I will not go near those animals,' he said. 'Kill them all!'

But at that moment, Hui, the boy who had once been a Shrike, came to us and spoke.

'Lord Tanus,' he said. 'I grew up in a land beyond the River Euphrates[82]. My people use horses to work in the fields. I know how to control them.'

So Tanus gave Hui a group of men to bring the horses and chariots to Thebes. They brought them down the west bank of the river while we sailed back to the capital in the boats.

We prepared to defend the part of our city which stood on the west bank of the Nile. We could not save the eastern part of Thebes. The Hyksos quickly captured it and they camped on the river bank. But they could not cross the river, so we thought that we had a little time to prepare our defence. Tanus made his camp in the half-built Palace of Memnon. It was not far from the tomb of Pharaoh Mamose.

I gave the body of Pharaoh to the priests of Anubis. They cut it open and removed the internal organs and the brain. They put the organs in canopic jars and they laid the body in a bath of special oils and herbs. Later, they wrapped the body in mummy cloths. But it was not safe to bury the body in the Valley of Kings. We knew that the Hyksos would cross the Nile one day and take the treasure from the tomb. So we brought Pharaoh's sarcophagus from the tomb which had been prepared for him.

Soon we learnt that the Hyksos had captured the fleet of

71

the false Pharaoh of the Delta. They had crossed the Nile far to the north, and now they were coming down the west bank towards us.

'We cannot stay here,' said Tanus. 'They will surround us and kill us.'

'Then we shall go south,' said Queen Lostris. 'We still have ships, so we can sail to the south. We will gather our people in the south and we will return to attack the Hyksos.'

'Perhaps that will be possible, my Lady,' I said. 'But I do not know how far we must go to escape the Hyksos.'

'We will travel as far as we need to,' said Tanus. 'The Nile is rising. We will be able to pull our ships through the cataract.'

And so we loaded all our boats with food and seeds and tools. We took the treasures of our Pharaoh and we took the body of Pharaoh himself in the gold sarcophagus.

These preparations took time, and we did not *have* much time. A large Hyksos army was marching towards us from the north. We had to burn everything that we could not carry. I was one of the last people in the camp, together with Tanus and Lostris, who was carrying Prince Memnon in her arms.

At last, we were ready to leave the camp in the half-built Palace of Memnon. We could see a great crowd of people on the river bank, waiting to get onto the ships. Suddenly they pointed to the north and started shouting.

'The Hyksos are here!' they shouted to the people who were already on the ships. 'Save yourselves!'

The ships started to move away from the bank. We were too late – we would not be able to reach the bank in time. Lostris had said, 'I will be the last person to leave my city. My people must be safe before I leave.' The people had gone now, but their Queen and their future Pharaoh were *not* safe.

Soon the Hyksos had surrounded the Palace of Memnon and were on the road to the river. Now we could only escape through the fields. But first, we had to get out of the palace.

The Hyksos entered the palace through the front gates as we were leaving by the back gate. There were two chariots with horses outside the back gate. There was only one guard with them. Tanus killed the guard and I lifted Lostris and Memnon into one of the chariots. I joined them and Tanus got into the second chariot.

'How do we drive these?' Tanus asked me.

'I don't know,' I replied. 'But we must find out quickly!'

Hui had already taught me something about horses. I lifted the reins[83] and the horses moved forward. The chariot gathered speed.

Suddenly, we saw two people running towards us. One of them was an archer, the other was Lord Intef. I drove my chariot straight at them.

'No!' shouted Lostris. 'He is my father.'

She shouted, but it was too late. The archer tried to shoot an arrow at us, then he jumped out of the way. But Lord Intef fell onto the knife on the hub of my chariot wheel. It caught in his body and the chariot dragged him along the road. He screamed as the knife cut his stomach open. Then we left him behind. I did not look back – I knew that he was dead.

I drove the horses along the flat river bank. Tanus's chariot was close behind us. We were just in time – the last ship was moving away from the bank. I pushed Lostris and Memnon onto the ship, and Tanus and I jumped on after them. We were safe for the moment.

————

But the Hyksos did not let us escape easily. Our ships moved slowly against the current and the Hyksos followed us along the banks of the river. If a ship came too close to the bank, the Hyksos shot arrows at us. We could not stop to rest, so our men took turns[84] to row and sleep. The Hyksos followed

73

us for twelve days.

The worst part of the journey was near Elephantine. Here the Nile passes through a narrow gorge[85] and our ships had to sail in a single line. The Hyksos climbed onto the cliffs above us and shot arrows and threw rocks down into the gorge. Many men, women and children were killed.

But the Hyksos did not follow us beyond Elephantine. We sailed to the First Cataract in safety, and there we stopped.

'To the south is the land of Cush,' I said. 'Few Egyptians have ever been to that land and returned. Here, we leave Egypt and go into the unknown country.'

Queen Lostris ordered me to carve a message into a large rock by the Nile. The message said —

> *I, Lostris, Queen of Egypt, will return to put my son*
> *on the throne of his country.*

When I carved those words, I expected to be back in Elephantine within a year or two. I had no idea how many long and difficult years would pass before we could return.

———

The water of the Nile was rising. The water began to cover the rocks of the cataract. We unloaded the ships and carried all the cargo on our backs up past the cataract. Then we pulled the ships through the cataract using ropes.

It was then that the Hyksos made their last attempt to catch us. They had rested in Elephantine for several days, because they believed it was impossible to take ships through the cataract.

All our ships were through the cataract by the time the Hyksos came up behind us. Now we were on the high ground and we fought off their attack. They did not follow us any further. But they now had the whole of Egypt for themselves.

———

74

We sailed to the First Cataract, and there we stopped.

We began our long journey into the unknown land. Most of our people now walked along the river bank and helped to pull the ships along. The Nile gave us water and fish. We found many animals along the banks, and we hunted those. But we saw no signs of men.

I kept a daily record of our journey. I found out the direction of our journey by watching the sun and the stars. I soon realized that, travelling on the river, we were moving towards the west rather than the south.

———

Months passed, and one day we came to a second cataract which was much more difficult and dangerous than the first. We had to wait for the water of the Nile to rise again before we could continue our journey. While we waited, our farmers planted crops in the rich earth along the river banks.

Here, there were many trees growing by the river, so I had plenty of wood to work with. I tried to copy some of the ideas of the Hyksos. I made wheels and I made simple chariots. Also, I had time to study a Hyksos bow which we had captured. It was not made from a single piece of wood. It was made of several thin pieces of wood joined together, and some pieces of animal horn. I made some copies of this bow. Although they were shorter than our own bows, they had greater power.

Where did I get the horn to make these bows? A large herd of the horned creatures called oryx[86] passed near us one day. We hunted them for food and I cut off their horns to use for the bows. Although he was only six years old, Prince Memnon came with us on the hunt. He wanted to come very much, although I said that he was too young.

'Your mother will kill me if you are injured,' I said.

He smiled at me but he would not change his mind. He was so like his mother.

Tanus watched over the young prince and all the soldiers

admired the boy. None of them suspected that he was the son of Tanus, although Memnon now had golden hair, like his real father.

12

The Prisoner of Arkoun

At last, the water of the Nile rose and we passed the Second Cataract. Then we journeyed for many months until we reached a third cataract. By now, a year and a half had passed since we had left Elephantine. But we had to wait until the river rose again before we could cross the Third Cataract and continue our journey.

As we travelled, I watched the stars and the sun. One day, I realized that the river had changed its direction and we were journeying towards the north. And after that, we came upon a huge fourth cataract. This Fourth Cataract was like a great sheet of falling water.

Our people began to complain. 'Where are we going?' they said. 'Will there be no end to our journey?'

I knew that we would not have to travel so far on our return journey. I made a map of the Nile and I showed it to Queen Lostris.

'When we return, we must leave the ships and cross the desert. In that way, we will travel from the Fourth Cataract to the Second Cataract in less than half the time,' I told her.

Queen Lostris told the people this news and then they stopped complaining. Kratus, who had escaped from Thebes too, decided to test my idea by crossing the desert to the Second Cataract with a few soldiers. It was a hard journey, but he returned in a month. My map was correct. There would be a quick way back to Egypt when we needed it.

———

When the river rose the next year, we crossed the Fourth Cataract. It was a difficult task and several men died. Then we journeyed on, and soon the river was taking us towards the south again. Now, instead of dry sand on the ground, we saw green plants everywhere. The skies were often covered with clouds, and rain often fell. Most of our people had never seen water fall from the sky before – it was a great surprise to them.

Three years had now passed since we had left Thebes. There was one more cataract to cross, but it was easier than the others. Then we had another surprise. We found out that there were *two* Niles – a dark river came from the east and a yellow river came from the south.

We stopped at the place where the two rivers met and we rested. We named the place Qebui. We stayed there for several years.

During this time, we met members of the local tribes[87] and we learnt much about this new land. These tribesmen told us that the dark river came from high mountains to the east. The yellow river came from an endless swamp where only insects and crocodiles could live.

During these years of exile[88], we carried the body of Pharaoh Mamose in its sarcophagus. Queen Lostris had not forgotten her promise to keep his body safe.

'I will build a tomb for my husband now,' she said. 'We must search in the mountains along the dark river. We must find a place for Pharaoh to rest.'

Tanus took some of the men, and he led them eastwards. I went with him and so did Prince Memnon.

We followed the dark river to the mountains. The river seemed to come down in steps from between huge dark cliffs. We saw storms in the mountains. We watched the lightning strike the rocks from the black clouds high above them. *This* was a place to build a tomb! No men ever came here. No one would ever find the place again.

As we returned to Qebui, we came across a huge herd of dark-coloured animals with small curved horns. They had long black and white hair on their chins. The local tribesmen told us these creatures were called *gnu*. We killed and cooked one of them. The meat tasted good.

When we got back to our camp, I told Lostris about these unusual animals. She sent out a group of hunters to kill some more of them and smoke their meat for the army. They also brought some gnu back to the camp alive.

By now we had bred many horses. But that year, something terrible happened. Half of our horses died because of a strange disease. The horses started coughing, and soon they were unable to breathe and they died. The tribesmen told me that the disease came from the gnu.

The disease never returned to the horses that survived. Nor did it come to the young horses that were born later. The horses had seemed to develop a protection from the disease.

———

During the next five years, we were able to increase our herd of horses again and we were able to train our army in new skills. We expected to return to Egypt one day, when we would have to fight the Hyksos. We made our preparations slowly and carefully.

I spent those five years supervising the building of Pharaoh's tomb. Eight thousand of the local tribesmen became our slaves. They moved the heavy rocks and prepared the place where the tomb would be built. The masons who had escaped with us from Thebes did the difficult work of carving the stone.

———

But there was a long interruption of my work on the tomb.

This is how it happened. One day, Prince Memnon and Tanus took some soldiers high up into the mountains. I went with them. By now, Prince Memnon was fourteen years old and he was a fine-looking young man.

We were still trying to find the beginning of the river. Where did the dark river start? We wanted to find out, but it was difficult to travel through the mountains.

We found an answer to our question in the rain. There were great storms in those mountains and a huge amount of rain fell on them. The rain ran down the mountains and made sudden floods in the valleys. The floods joined and became the river.

One day, one of these sudden floods knocked us all off our feet. Our men were separated and I was nearly drowned. At the end of that day, only Tanus and Memnon were still with me. We spent a bad night among the trees on the mountainside.

At dawn we realized that we were lost. But we saw some smoke rising from a valley and went towards it.

The river ran through the valley and we saw a group of brightly-coloured tents near the river. As we approached, we saw men near the tents. They had black curly hair and they carried knives in their belts.

'These are not simple people,' said Tanus. 'They have knives. They are clever metal workers.'

'Look, there beyond the tents,' I said. 'They have horses too.'

We saw a number of strong horses, larger than our own animals.

'If we can bring some of those to our own herd, we will breed bigger horses,' said Tanus.

Suddenly, were surprised by a shout. Looking round, I saw that Prince Memnon had gone closer to the river on his own. He had found a group of women who were bathing in the water. Memnon was staring at a beautiful naked girl and the girl was staring back at him. Later, I learnt that they fell in love with each other at that moment. Memnon spoke to her, but she did not understand him. The women started to scream and the men ran from the tents.

'We must escape!' shouted Tanus. Memnon, Tanus and I started to run along the bank of the river. Arrows fell all around us and suddenly I felt a sharp pain in my leg.

'Leave me!' I called to the other two. 'I am wounded.'

But Tanus would not leave me and he ran back to me. At the same time, a large man with a black beard ran along the bank towards us. He carried a big sword made of light-blue metal. Tanus took out his own sword and prepared to fight. The bearded man swung his sword at Tanus. Tanus lifted his own sword and the two weapons clashed together. Then Tanus stared at his sword in astonishment – it was cut in half!

'Run!' I said. 'Save Memnon.'

Tanus knew what his duty was – to guard the future Pharaoh. He ran after Memnon. I was taken prisoner.

The curly-haired man pulled me back to his camp. I could not walk because of the arrow in my leg. All the men in the camp looked at me and they talked loudly in a language which I had never heard.

While they were talking, I carefully removed the arrow from my leg. The men watched me closely. I had the skills of a healer and they could see this, so they did not kill me. They let me live because they needed a healer for their people. And that day, I was taken to a village on a hill where I lived with the curly-haired people for some months.

I learn things quickly, and I listened carefully to the curly-haired people's language. Soon I could understand their words. I found out that we were in the kingdom of Askum.

*Memnon was staring at a beautiful naked girl and the girl was
staring back at him.*

The people were called Geez and their leader's name was Arkoun. I used my skills to heal several of the villagers and they were kind to me, although they guarded me day and night.

The kingdom of Aksum was a strange place. It was a land where men fought each other for pleasure.

One day, I saw again the young girl who had been bathing in the river. She, too, was a prisoner of Arkoun. Her father was Arkoun's neighbour, a man called Prester Beni-Jon. Arkoun had captured Prester Beni-Jon's daughter, whose name was Masara, because the two men hated each other. Both Arkoun and Prester Beni-Jon called themselves 'King of Kings in the land of Aksum'. I wanted to show them an Egyptian Pharaoh – then they would know what 'King of Kings' really meant!

———

After some time, Arkoun and his people left the village and travelled to Adbar Seged. Adbar Seged was a small stronghold on the top of a mountain. The only way into the stronghold of Adbar Seged was a narrow bridge across a very deep gorge. When I looked down from the bridge, I felt dizzy. It was a terrible sight! It was a long way to the bottom of the gorge. I learnt that if anyone made Arkoun angry, his soldiers threw them from the bridge.

One morning, I was told that Masara was sick. My skill as a healer would be needed. I was taken to her room, which was a comfortable cell high up in the fortress. She lay on a bed, and she was crying. I asked her guards to leave us while I talked to her.

'What is wrong?' I asked her.

She stopped crying and smiled at me.

'Nothing is wrong,' she answered. 'I wanted to talk to you.'

'What about?'

'About the golden-haired boy who I saw by the river.

83

Who is he and what did he say to me?'

And so I told her about Prince Memnon. I told her about the land of Egypt and about our long journey.

'You must escape from here and go to my father,' said Masara. 'He will help you return to your people, then you can bring Prince Memnon here to rescue me. When you escape, tell the Prince that I love him.'

On that day, escape seemed impossible, and for several years it *was* impossible. But I did escape in the end, and this is how it happened. When Arkoun led his men in a battle with Prester Beni-Jon's people, I went with them as Arkoun's healer. He wanted me with him in case he was wounded in the battle.

As we rode out of Adbar Seged across the narrow bridge, I asked Arkoun about his blue sword. I was interested in the sword that had cut Tanus's bronze sword in half. Arkoun's sword was made from a metal which was stronger than bronze. Was it the same metal that the Hyksos made their weapons from? I wanted to know about it. But Arkoun told me that he did not know what metal his sword was made from. His grandfather had received it from a god, he said.

———

The battle was a strange one. It had been carefully arranged. The two sides had agreed a time and a place to fight. Prester Beni-Jon and his men were waiting for us there.

Prester Beni-Jon was a tall, thin man with a long white beard. He came forward a few steps and shouted at Arkoun. Arkoun went forward a few steps and shouted back at him. Then several other soldiers took turns to shout at each other. Finally there was a little fighting. I fell asleep until the battle was over. One side had won, I was told when I woke, but I did not understand *how*!

Seven men had been wounded in the fighting, and one of Arkoun's men was badly hurt. I looked after him as we started to return to Adbar Seged. I carried him on my horse.

On the way, we crossed a fast-flowing stream. In the middle of the stream, my horse slipped. The strong current carried me and the wounded man down the stream.

I escaped from Arkoun! But I became a prisoner of Prester Beni-Jon instead! As soon as I got out of the water, I was captured by more curly-headed, black-bearded men and taken to the *other* King of Kings of the land of Aksum.

Prester Beni-Jon looked both kind and dangerous. Fortunately, he understood me when I spoke to him in the Geez language. I was able to give him news about his daughter, Masara, who was a prisoner in Adbar Seged. He was pleased to hear about his daughter, but he was worried too.

'Arkoun wants too much gold for her,' he said. 'And I cannot attack Adbar Seged. It is impossible for my men to cross that narrow bridge without being seen. They could only cross it a few at a time, and when they reached the other side, they would be killed by Arkoun's men.'

'I can help you,' I told him. 'If you send me back to my own people, I will bring many soldiers to attack Arkoun.'

Prester Beni-Jon was interested in my idea. But we talked about it for two days, before he agreed to it.

13

The Tomb in the Mountains

When I returned to my people at Qebui, Prince Memnon had changed a lot. He was now seventeen years old and he looked very much like his father had looked as a young man. As I watched the prince, I remembered another day, twenty years before. I thought of the day of the hippopotamus hunt on the River Nile. Time, like the river, moves on. Tanus himself was growing old now. His golden hair was turning grey. And Lostris was now a middle-aged woman. She had lost some teeth, but she was still beautiful.

'Taita,' she said when she saw me. 'We are so happy to see you. We thought that you were dead.'

I told my story and I explained my arrangement with Prester Beni-Jon. 'His people will guard the tomb of Pharaoh Mamose for us for ever,' I said. 'And he will give us many strong horses. If we capture the stronghold of Adbar Seged for Prester Beni-Jon and rescue his daughter, all of Arkoun's treasures will be ours.'

Memnon became very excited at our plans to rescue Prester Beni-Jon's daughter. He had not forgotten Masara and he asked me many questions about her. When I told Memnon about Masara's message of love, he was very happy.

And so we moved our Egyptian army up into the mountains. Arkoun had many spies in the land and he knew that we were coming. Some of his archers attacked us on the way. But they did not stop us. We had copied the powerful bows of the Hyksos and we could shoot arrows further than any of Arkoun's archers.

We reached the gorge in front of Adbar Seged. There was a village there near the bridge. This village and the bridge to the stronghold were guarded by many men. Soon I had a plan.

I dressed a small group of our soldiers in clothes like the ones that the people of Aksum wore. I covered their heads with false hair which we had made from the tails of our horses. Then, as most of our army attacked the village, I led the small group – which included Prince Memnon – to the bridge.

'We are under King Arkoun's orders,' I shouted in Geez to

the guards at the bridge. The guards at the bridge moved aside for us and we crossed the bridge safely. When we entered Adbar Seged, we found that there were no guards in the town at all. All of Arkoun's soldiers were on the other side of the bridge, ready to defend it.

We went straight to Masara's cell. Prince Memnon took off the false hair that covered his head. He stared at Masara with love in his eyes.

'You've come back,' she said simply. I could understand what she said, though Memnon could not. But her face told him what she meant.

'Take care of her, Taita,' Memnon said. 'I'll go to the bridge!'

I stayed in the cell with Masara while Memnon and the other soldiers went back to the bridge. The rest of our army had now arrived at the gorge, and Arkoun's men were attacked from both sides. They tried to close the gates to the bridge but Memnon stopped them. Tanus led the rest of our army across the bridge to Adbar Seged.

But suddenly, Arkoun himself was standing at the end of the bridge. He ran at Tanus and thrust his blue sword at my friend. Tanus stopped the sword with his shield. The sword was very strong and sharp, and the end of it passed straight through the shield. But the sword was trapped there!

As Arkoun tried to pull it out, Tanus jumped forward and pushed Arkoun backwards. The King of Kings fell over the edge of the bridge, and down into the gorge. He screamed as he fell a thousand feet to the rocks below. When the soldiers of Adbar Seged saw that their king was dead, they stopped fighting.

Tanus walked towards me. I saw that the sword of Arkoun had been pushed right through his shield.

'Now I have the blue sword,' he said. And those were the last words he ever spoke. As he fell to the ground, I saw that the sword of Arkoun had entered his chest. A moment later, Tanus, Lord Harrab, Great Lion of Egypt, was dead.

Tanus jumped forward and pushed Arkoun backwards.

We carried Tanus's body back to Qebui. We embalmed his body and soon it lay next to the body of Pharaoh Mamose. The two bodies lay in a cave while we finished our work on the great tomb in the mountains. Pharaoh Mamose lay in his golden sarcophagus and Tanus lay in a painted wooden coffin.

One night, I did something which only one other person knows about. This is my most terrible secret, and I have many secrets. That night, with the help of Kratus, I changed the body of Pharaoh with the body of Tanus. They were both wrapped in mummy cloths. We took the body of Tanus out of its wooden coffin and put it in the royal sarcophagus. The body of Pharaoh Mamose went into the simple wooden coffin of Tanus.

And so, when at last Queen Lostris led us into the high mountains for the funeral ceremonies, we buried Pharaoh in the tomb we had prepared for Tanus. And we carried Tanus, in the golden sarcophagus, into the great secret tomb which we had prepared for Pharaoh. He will lie there forever.

I was the last person to leave the tomb. I put Lanata, the great bow of Tanus, on top of the sarcophagus and I put a little statue of myself next to it. The statue showed me as a scribe. There were words carved on its base —

I am Taita. I am your friend. I will answer for you.

I promised that I would speak to the gods and tell them of all the good things Tanus had done. I hope to see Tanus in the Afterlife. But there in the secret chamber, I said goodbye to him for the last time in this world. Then we sealed the tomb. We built traps to kill tomb thieves, but the entrance to the tomb will never be found. I hid it too well.

Then we left the mountains, and after that day, Lostris was never well again. She lost all joy in living – she couldn't bear to live without Tanus.

———

Memnon chose Masara, daughter of Prester Beni-Jon, as his wife. Queen Lostris did not want her son to marry a Cushite[89]. But in the end, she accepted her son's choice. Memnon and Masara were married by both Cushite and Egyptian priests.

'I have lived to see my son marry,' said Lostris. 'Now I have one more thing to do. I shall return my people to the land of Egypt, and then I shall die in the city where I was born. I shall die in the city of Thebes.'

14

We Return to Egypt

The day after the royal wedding, we began our return to Egypt. It took us two years. By the time we reached the First Cataract – the one near Elephantine– I knew that my mistress was dying. Her hair was now the colour of silver and she had a dreadful pain in her stomach all the time. She could not eat. I prepared medicine from the seeds of poppy plants[90]. It made Lostris's pain less and it helped her to sleep.

We crossed from the land of Cush into the land of Egypt. We stopped at the rock which I had carved, so many years before. We read the words —

I, Lostris, Queen of Egypt, will return to put my son on the throne of his country.

When she saw these words, Lostris smiled and nodded her head. She had kept her promise to Pharaoh Mamose and she had kept her promise to the people of Egypt.

———

We sent spies along the river. They reported that the Hyksos were still strong. The King of the Hyksos had rebuilt the towns that had been destroyed. He had an army of twelve thousand chariots and many more soldiers on foot. His army was much larger than ours.

But I had a plan. I had brought many of those strange animals called gnu from the land of Cush. Once, they had nearly destroyed our herd of horses – now I expected them to destroy the horses of the Hyksos.

First we captured Elephantine. This was not difficult because we surprised the Hyksos – they were not expecting us to come. Our army surrounded the city at night and we captured their ships. Many Egyptians, who were slaves of the Hyksos, welcomed us back. They threw open the gates of the city and the Hyksos ran away.

Most of the Hyksos soldiers were in Lower Egypt. They did not expect an attack from the south. They ruled the country from Memphis. This surprised me.

I was also surprised that the Egyptians of Elephantine turned against the Hyksos so quickly. The Hyksos had been their masters for twenty years, but they were still hated.

Soon there was a Pharaoh in Upper Egypt again. Memnon stopped using the name he was given at birth, and from that time he was called Pharaoh Tamose.

Pharaoh Tamose put on the double crown of Egypt and carried the crook and the flail of a king. The people knelt in front of him as they had knelt in front of Mamose. News of his return went swiftly down the river to Memphis.

The older Egyptians remembered Queen Lostris, although they did not recognize her now. Because she was very ill, she looked older than she really was. She could no longer walk and she was carried everywhere.

Our spies told us that the Hyksos king had heard about our army and was beginning to gather his own soldiers. He was preparing to travel south with ten thousand chariots and fifty thousand horses.

I put my gnu in a field with a hundred of the Hyksos' horses which we had captured at Elephantine. I left the animals together long enough to be sure that the gnu passed their disease to all the horses. Then Hui, who was now a great leader, put the horses onto a ship and we sailed to Thebes. We took with us some young Egyptian sailors who had grown up since the Hyksos came to the land. They could speak the Hyksos language.

We reached Thebes at sunset. Our sailors answered the questions of the guards at the wharf. They told the guards that our horses were from Asyut and the Hyksos guards let us enter the city. After all, we were bringing horses to Thebes, not taking them away!

There were a lot of troops and horses in the city. We were not noticed among so many men and animals. We took our diseased horses to the great stables of the city and we left them there.

The next day, we sailed back to Elephantine and found that Pharaoh Tamose and his army were ready to march towards Thebes. Pharaoh moved his main army along the east bank of the Nile and sent a smaller number of men along the other side of the river. We did not really have enough men or chariots or horses or ships. But the small fleet of ships moved along the river beside us.

That day, Pharaoh Tamose wore the War Crown of Egypt and he carried the blue sword of Arkoun. He looked so much like Tanus when he was a young man. Lostris noticed this and she smiled as we carried her down to the east bank of the river. At last, she was going home.

———

Apachan, King of the Hyksos, was waiting for us at Thebes. He had moved his army swiftly by land. They had camped on the plain below the city, and they moved to take up their battle positions as our army approached.

Pharaoh spoke to me as we looked at the Hyksos army.

'Can you guess their numbers, Taita?'

'There are only half the number of soldiers that I expected,' I replied. 'My spies told me that there is sickness in the Hyksos camp. Their horses are dying from the gnu disease.'

'I hope that you're right,' said Pharaoh Tamose. 'If Apachan has more soldiers than these, he may have a plan to attack us on the flanks or from the rear.'

I looked at him with admiration. He was so much like his father. Although he had never seen a great battle, he had learned much from Tanus. Our men trusted him, as they had trusted his father.

We did not have time to make many preparations for the battle because the Hyksos quickly started to attack us. Their army was between us and Thebes.

Most of our soldiers were young, but they were not untrained. We had practised fighting with chariots during the years of our long exile. I had also copied the Hyksos bows and our archers were now as good as theirs. Our foot soldiers knew that they must not be worried by the horses and chariots. If they ran, they would be killed. If they stood still, with their spears pointing forwards, our archers could keep the chariots away from them. We could move forward and push the Hyksos from the battlefield.

The Hyksos attacked us with chariots. They still remembered the battle of Abnub and they expected us to run away. But our men stood still. Our archers killed the Hyksos horses at the front. Meanwhile our own chariots passed the Hyksos on the right, then turned to attack them on the flanks and at the rear. Now it was the turn of the Hyksos to run away!

We marched towards the Hyksos camp on the plain of Thebes. The city was to our left and our ships were already attacking

The Hyksos army was between us and Thebes.

the wharfs.

But the Hyksos soldiers had made strong defences for their camp. They gathered behind walls of wood and spears, where our chariots could not follow them. Our army began to spread out across the plain of Thebes to surround the camp.

Then the gates of Thebes opened. Apachan, the Hyksos king, had kept many soldiers inside the city. Now they attacked our left flank.

Pharaoh saw the Hyksos chariots appear on our left flank. He gave orders at once.

'Follow me!' he called to his own chariots. He led the attack against the Hyksos. On that day, I was Pharaoh's chariot driver. I had not expected to be in the battle, but I had no choice. We raced towards the Hyksos lines.

The War Crown made Pharaoh Tamose a target for the Hyksos. It was a target that brought Apachan himself towards us. He wanted to be the person who killed the Egyptian pharaoh. His other chariots stayed back for a moment.

The King of the Hyksos was a big man. He shot two arrows at us. Tamose caught one of them on his shield. Then Apachan's chariot rushed straight at us, and in a moment it was next to our chariot. The King swung his sword at Tamose's head and he shouted with a terrible voice. Tamose pushed aside the Hyksos sword and then thrust the point of his blue sword between the teeth of the Hyksos king, right to the back of his throat. Blood gushed from the wound.

The King of the Hyksos dropped his sword and held the side of his chariot. His driver turned the chariot and drove it back towards the gates of Thebes. The Hyksos king was dying, and the gates were shut against him.

The people of Thebes had turned against the Hyksos and they closed the gates as soon as their soldiers had ridden out of the city. They would not open them again when the Hyksos army tried to return to escape the anger of our soldiers.

Some of the Hyksos soldiers tried to reach their camp on the plain. Others ran for the boats on the river. Our army and navy were waiting for them. They killed thousands of the Hyksos that day.

Kratus and the men that he commanded chased the Hyksos until late in the afternoon, then they returned to the Egyptian camp. The bodies of the dead and the dying lay all over the plain of Thebes. I remembered the Battle of Abnub. This was another massacre, but this time the bodies were of Hyksos men, not Egyptians. This time, the Hyksos army was destroyed.

At the end of the day, Pharaoh gave orders for our wounded men to be looked after. Then he entered Thebes. He entered the city wearing the double crown and carrying the crook and the flail. The hundred gates of Thebes opened to the new King of Egypt.

'Hail Pharaoh. May you live forever! Hail Pharaoh. May you live forever!' the people of the city shouted.

Pharaoh Tamose went immediately to the Temple of Osiris at Karnak. But Queen Lostris was carried into Thebes secretly. She was ill and weak, and she did not want the people to see her. Lostris was still a Queen, but she was no longer ruler of Egypt. Now there was a new Pharaoh.

That evening, Lostris asked to be taken to the Palace of Memnon on the west bank. Her room faced the east, towards the light of dawn. We laid the Queen on a bed and she looked out of the window at the dark night sky.

'Taita, I want to be alone with you,' she said to me. I sent the guards and servants away. Now we spoke quietly together.

Lostris had known me when she was a child in the house of her father. She had told me that her first memory was of me. I had taken care of her then. Now she wanted me to take care of her again, for the last time.

She was in terrible pain, and I knew that the poppy seed

97

medicine could no longer help her. But she did sleep for a while. As she slept, I held her hand.

When she awoke, in the darkness before dawn, she cried out.

'The pain! Sweet Isis, help me – the pain!'

Then, after a little while, she spoke again. 'The pain has gone now, but I feel so cold. Hold me, Taita. Warm me.'

So I held my mistress in my arms, as I had held her when she was a child, and I sang softly to her.

Then she spoke for the last time. 'I have loved only two men in my life, Taita. And one of them was you.'

She felt so cold in my arms. I held her tightly. I could not bear to let her go.

'Goodbye, my love,' I whispered. 'Farewell, my heart.'

———

I have written these scrolls for the Tomb of Queen Lostris. They will remain with her and they will tell the story of her life. I wish to remain here too. Perhaps, in the Afterlife, the gods will treat us more kindly.

I am Taita
Slave of Lostris, Queen of Egypt

I held my mistress in my arms, as I had held her when she was a child.

Points for Understanding

1

'Lostris was a prisoner,' Taita says. Why does he say this?

2

'Your father will kill me,' Taita tells Lostris. Why does he think this?

3

1 'I will give you a chance to explain what happened,' Lord Intef tells Taita. Why does he think that Taita has not told him everything about the hunt?
2 Why did the people of Thebes give the north wind a new name?

4

1 Taita's masons had not done their work well, but Taita would not be angry with them. Why not?
2 'Isn't Tanus wonderful?' Lostris says to Taita at the end of the play. Taita does not answer her. Why not?

5

Taita talks to Kratus. He is shocked by Kratus's news. Why? What does he think about Tanus's behaviour?

6

'You have surprised me,' Tanus tells Taita. Why does he say this?

7

1 Why does Taita return to Jebel Nagara with a cargo of women's clothes?
2 How does Taita help Tanus at the battle in the temple at Gallala?

8

1 Pharaoh thinks that Taita has returned from the dead. Taita wants him to go on thinking this. Why do you think Taita wants this?
2 Taita says that he made use of his 'special powers'. What does he mean by this?

9

Why are Mamose's soldiers now strong enough to attack the army of the false Pharaoh?

10

The Egyptians get several surprises at the battle of Abnub. List three of them.

11

1 In this chapter, Taita makes use of several of the surprises he had at the Battle of Abnub. How does he do this?
2 Taita thinks that Memnon is very like his mother. When Memnon will not change his mind about the hunt, what do you think Taita remembers?

12

Why do Arkoun's men not kill Taita?

13

Why do you think that Taita puts Tanus's body in Pharaoh's sarcophagus?

14

1 Why has Taita brought gnu back to Egypt with him?
2 What have the Egyptian soldiers learnt during their exile which helps them fight the Hyksos?

Glossary

1 **papyrus scrolls** (page 4)
   the Ancient Egyptians often wrote their records on *papyrus*, a kind of paper made from *papyrus reeds* – tall plants which grow in the shallow water along the edges of rivers and lakes.
2 **slave** (page 5)
   someone who is not free because they are owned by another person. Slaves have to work for their owners, who give them food and somewhere to live but do not pay them. At the time of this story, slaves were often people from an enemy country who were captured in battle.
3 **swiftly** (page 5)
   to move *swiftly* means to move very quickly. If a person or a thing moves very quickly, they, or it, can be described as *swift*.
4 **tomb** (page 8)
   another word for a grave – a place where a dead body is buried or stored. It usually means a building of some kind, rather than a simple hole in the ground. The Ancient Egyptians believed in life after death – the Afterlife. So the pharaohs built magnificent tombs for themselves. They filled the tombs with treasure and all the things they would use in the Afterlife.

5 **twin cities** (page 8)

cities that are as equally important as each other. They are the same size and have similar numbers of people living in them. Thebes and Karnak were close beside each other on the Nile. Thebes was on the west bank of the Nile and was the capital city of Upper Egypt. The Governor of Upper Egypt lived in a palace there. On the east bank of the river, there was the huge Temple of Osiris at Karnak. The Pharaoh of Upper Egypt lived in a palace at Elephantine, an island on the River Nile.

6 **crops** (page 9)

plants which are grown to eat. For example, corn, wheat, maize or rice.

7 **bow** (page 9)

the *bow* [baʊ] of a boat is the front part of it. The back part of a boat is the *stern*. The verb *to bow* [baʊ] means to bend your head forward, or to bend the upper part of your body forward, as a sign of respect to somebody who is more powerful or important than you. There is another noun *bow* [bəʊ], which means a weapon. (See Glossary Number 14.)

8 **hippopotamuses** (page 9)

very large animals, with thick grey skin, which live in or near rivers and lakes. They have short legs, wide bodies and large heads with very wide mouths.

9 **rebellion** (page 12)

when a group of people disagree with a ruler or a government, and work together to change or replace that ruler or government, they are *rebelling* against him or it. Their action is called a *rebellion*.

10 **bands** (page 13)

a group of people who do something together can be called a *band*. The word is often used for a group of criminals. Note: do not confuse this general sense of the word with the special sense where *band* means a group of musicians who play together.

11 **merchants** (page 13)

people who buy and sell things to earn money. Merchants are also called *traders*, and they earn money by *trading*.

12 **Blue Crocodile Guard** (page 13)

this group of soldiers takes its name from the *crocodile* – an animal like a very large lizard which lives in rivers and lakes in hot, wet parts of the world. Crocodiles are very dangerous. They have strong bodies and tails, and long jaws with very sharp teeth. In Ancient Egypt, crocodiles were respected, and several Egyptian gods were pictured in the form of a crocodile.

103

13 **lookout** (page 14)

someone who stands at the front of a ship, or on high ground near a soldiers' camp. Lookouts watch for other ships, other soldiers, or – as in this case – animals which are being hunted.

14 **bow** (page 14)

a weapon which shoots arrows. It is made from a long, thin strip of a strong material, usually wood, which is pulled into a curve by a string tied between its ends.

15 **mistress** (page 14)

the female form of the word *master*, a term of respect.

16 **surfaced** – *to surface* (page 15)

if something or someone has been under the surface of water or some other liquid, and then rises to the surface, it or they have *surfaced*.

17 **creature** (page 15)

another word for animal.

18 **thrust** – *to thrust* (page 15)

to push with great force.

19 **Osiris** (page 17)

one of the chief gods of the Ancient Egyptian religion. The Egyptians thought that after their death, they went to live in an underworld, where – if they had been good people – they had an *Afterlife*. They thought that Osiris ruled this underworld. In sculptures, carvings and paintings, Osiris is usually pictured as a handsome man, wearing a tall crown. (See page 111.)

20 **Hapi** (page 18)

the god of the yearly floods of the Nile, rather than of the river itself. Hapi is usually pictured as a man with river plants on his head. (See page 111.) Sometimes he has both male and female features.

21 **smoked and salted** (page 19)

smoking and *salting* are two ways of preserving raw meat – keeping it so that it can be eaten a long time after the animal has been killed. Pieces of meat are *smoked* by hanging them over a fire for some hours, or even days, so that the smoke from the fire preserves and flavours them. Pieces of meat are *salted* by being packed tightly in a container with a lot of salt.

22 **wharf** (page 19)

a place where ships are loaded and unloaded, or where people get on and off them.

23 **fell to my knees** – *to fall to your knees* (page 22)
   if you kneel on the ground in front of a king or some other important person, you are *falling to your knees*. 'Fall' is not meant literal-
   ly here.

24 **innocent** (page 22)
   here, the word does not mean the opposite of 'guilty' (of a crime).
   It means that Lostris is a virgin – she has not had sexual intercourse
   with Tanus, or anyone else.

25 **Isis** (page 22)
   one of the most important Egyptian goddesses, and the sister and
   wife of Osiris. She is often pictured as a beautiful woman wearing a
   crown made of a pair of cow's horns with the sun between them.
   (See page 111.)

26 **escort** – *to escort* (page 22)
   to *escort* someone from one place to another means to go with
   them, and to guard them.

27 **barge** (page 23)
   a kind of large boat with a flat bottom.

28 **Eye of Horus** (page 23)
   Horus was one of the most important Egyptian gods. He was the
   son of Isis and Osiris. He was believed to be the protector of the
   kings of Egypt. He is sometimes pictured with a man's body and the
   head of a fierce bird – a falcon. (See page 111.) Sometimes he is
   pictured simply as a falcon who wears a crown. In many of the
   stories about the gods, Horus is attacked and wounded by his brother Seth. In one of these stories, Seth cuts out Horus's eyes. But
   another god repairs the damage and Horus goes on fighting his
   evil brother. Because of this, Horus, as the defender of the kings of
   Egypt, is often pictured as a single eye. Tanus's boat is called the
   Eye of Horus, because Tanus protects the Pharaoh. (See the illustration on pages 10 and 111.)

29 **throne** (page 23)
   a special kind of chair in which kings and other rulers sit. Thrones
   are usually made of gold and precious jewels.

30 **make-up** (page 23)
   paint which you put on your face. Rich Ancient Egyptians often
   put white make-up over their faces and black make-up around
   their eyes.

31 **Delta** (page 23)
   the area of northern Egypt where the Nile meets the sea. The river
   divides into many smaller streams here. These streams and the

coast, if seen from above, make a shape like the Greek letter *delta* (Δ). In this book, the Delta means the same as Lower Egypt.

32 **current** (page 24)
when the water in a river or the sea flows strongly in one direction, this is called a *current*.

33 **bowed my head** (page 25)
see Glossary Number 7.

34 **supervised** – *to supervise* (page 25)
if you control the work of a group of people, you are *supervising* them – you are their *supervisor*. Your job is to make sure that the quality of their work is high.

35 **part** – *to have, take, or play, a part* (page 25)
when an actor in a play pretends to be one of the characters in that play, he is *taking*, or *playing*, the *part* of that character. In this play, Tanus is going to *play the part* of the god Horus.

36 **masons** (page 26)
skilful workers who carve and shape stone for building.

37 **torches** (page 26)
things for making light in dark places. In this story, the torches are long, thin sticks of wood with bundles of burning plants at the top.

38 **a dead man** – *to be a dead man* (page 30)
an idiom used to threaten someone. If you say to someone, 'You are a dead man!' you mean, 'I am going to kill you!' Here Taita means, 'I was sure that Lord Intef would kill Tanus.'

39 **rid** – *to rid someone or something of someone or something* (page 30)
if you take something unwanted or harmful away from someone, you *rid* that person of that thing.

40 **silt** (page 32)
mud or sand which is carried from one place to another by a river.

41 **flail and crook** (page 32)
things which the pharaohs of Egypt carried to show their power – the *symbols* of their power. A *flail* is a wooden tool. It is used to separate the usable parts of crop plants from the unusable parts by beating the plants. A *crook* is a long stick with a hook on the end. It is used to control animals, especially sheep. (See the illustrations on pages 34 and 111.)

42 **squares** (page 32)
areas of land of an exact, measured size.

43 **hooded cobra** (page 35)
a very dangerous kind of snake. If it bites someone, the poison which it puts into the person's skin can kill them.

44 **disguise** (page 36)

when you put on clothes which are not your own, so that you look like someone else, you are wearing a *disguise*.

45 **tavern** (page 37)

a place where people meet together. They can buy food and drink there.

46 **irrigation channels** (page 38)

small straight streams that have been dug in the ground. They lead water from the river to the fields so that the crops are *irrigated*.

47 **swamps** (page 38)

areas of very wet ground.

48 **ashamed** (page 39)

if you do something which you know you should not have done, and you are sorry about doing it, you are *ashamed*. You can *look ashamed*, or you can *be ashamed of* doing something.

49 **exhausted** (page 43)

very tired, so that you have no strength in your body and find it difficult to move.

50 **healer** (page 44)

someone who makes sick people well is a *healer*.

51 **cargo** (page 44)

things which are carried in a trading ship – a ship owned by a merchant – are that ship's *cargo*.

52 **Baron** (page 46)

a leader who is not a chief leader. He controls many people, but he is controlled by a more important leader.

53 **oasis** (page 48)

a place in a very dry area where water can be found and plants grow.

54 **advanced on** – *to advance on something or someone* (page 48)

if people move towards something, they are *advancing on it*. The expression is usually used when talking about soldiers and armies.

55 **target** (page 49)

a *target* is something that you shoot at, with a gun or a bow and arrow. An *easy target*, is something – usually a person or an animal – which you can hit easily with your bullet or arrow.

56 **massacre** (page 49)

if a very large number of people are killed in a battle, this is a *massacre*. The word usually means that a large number of people on one side in a battle have been killed while only a few people on the other side have died.

107

57 **survivors** (page 50)

people who are not killed in a battle or in an accident. They have *survived* that battle, or accident.

58 **quarters** (page 51)

the rooms or buildings where the slaves live are the slaves' *quarters*.

59 **starving** (page 51)

if you are ill or dying because you have not eaten anything, you are *starving*.

60 **Anubis** (page 53)

the Egyptian god of tombs and embalming – the preparation of dead bodies for their tombs. Anubis is an important god in the underworld where Osiris rules. Anubis is often pictured as a desert dog – a jackal. But he is also pictured with a man's body and a jackal's head. (See page 111.)

61 **stronghold** (page 54)

a castle or a strongly-defended town. A place where people are safe from their enemies.

62 **promoted** – *to promote someone* (page 54)

if you give someone a more important job than the one they already have, you are *promoting* them.

63 **court** (page 55)

a ruler and all the people who live and work with him or her are called a *court*.

64 **gazelles** (page 55)

animals which run and jump very quickly and beautifully. They are a kind of small deer.

65 **shelter** – *to shelter* (page 55)

if you hide from bad weather, you are *sheltering from* it. You are also *taking shelter* from it, or *sheltering*. There is also a noun, a *shelter*, which means the place where you hide. You usually shelter in a building of some kind, but not always. You can also shelter behind a rock, under a tree, or in a cave.

66 **made love** – *to make love to someone* (page 57)

here 'make love to her' means, 'have sexual intercourse with her'.

67 **sarcophagus** (page 58)

a large, decorated container for a dead body. It is made of carved stone, or gold, or some other metal. In Ancient Egypt, the body of an important person was usually put in a sarcophagus. Often the body was contained in a painted wooden coffin, which was then put inside the sarcophagus.

68 **canopic jars** (page 58)

when important people died in Ancient Egypt, their internal organs – lungs, liver, stomach and intestines – were removed from their bodies. These organs were put into *canopic jars* – decorated pottery or stone jars. The jars were put into the tomb separately from the body. There were always four canopic jars, and their lids were usually sculptures of the heads of the four gods who protected the organs. These were the four sons of the great god Horus – Duamutef, Imsety, Hapi and Qebehsenuef. (See the illustration on page 111.)

69 **The Book of the Dead** (page 59)

the book which contained the Ancient Egyptian funeral ceremony. Important people had their own special copy of the book which was put into their tomb. The pictures in the book showed the dead person being received into the underworld by Anubis and led by him to Osiris.

70 **mummy cloths** (page 59)

the bodies of important Egyptians were tightly wrapped in long pieces of cloth containing special oils and herbs. These helped to preserve the bodies, so that they did not rot and fall into pieces. A body which was wrapped in this way was called a *mummy*.

71 **fleets** (page 62)

a *fleet* is a large number of ships.

72 **suspected** – *to suspect* (page 62)

if you think that someone is doing something wrong, you *suspect* them of doing that thing, or *suspect that* they are doing it.

73 **warriors** (page 65)

people who fight in wars – soldiers.

74 **War Council** (page 65)

the people who give Pharaoh advice about fighting wars – soldiers and other advisers – are his *War Council*.

75 **ranks** (page 65)

rows of soldiers who stand side by side.

76 **gathered speed** – *to gather speed* (page 67)

started slowly, then moved faster and faster.

77 **flanks** (page 67)

the soldiers on the ends of the ranks are the *flanks* of the army.

78 **hub** (page 67)

the centre of a wheel.

79 **'Form the tortoise'** (page 69)

Tanus is telling his men to stand closely round Pharaoh and hold up their shields. The shields will protect Pharaoh, as a tortoise's shell protects the animal inside it.

80 **wail** – *to wail* (page 69)

to weep loudly.

81 **breed** – *to breed something* (page 71)

when you keep animals and arrange for the males to make the females pregnant, so that they produce young animals, you are *breeding* those animals.

82 **River Euphrates** (page 71)

the long river which flows through the present-day countries of Turkey, Syria and Iraq. It is far to the east of Egypt.

83 **reins** (page 73)

long straps, attached to a piece of metal in a horse's mouth. Reins are used to turn the animal to the left or right, or to stop it.

84 **took turns** – *to take turns* (page 74)

when a number of people do a job one after another, they are *taking turns* to do it. Here, some people row while others sleep. Then the sleepers wake and row, while the people who have been rowing go to sleep.

85 **gorge** (page 74)

a deep narrow valley, often with a river running through it.

86 **oryx** (page 76)

a large animal like a deer. It has two long curved horns on its head.

87 **local tribes** (page 78)

groups of people who live together, come from the same place, and believe the same things.

88 **exile** (page 78)

if you are forced to leave the country where you live, you are *going into exile* – you have been *exiled*. The time you have to spend in another country is called your *exile*.

89 **Cushite** (page 90)

someone who was born in the land of *Cush*.

90 **poppy plants** (page 90)

poppy plants have brightly-coloured flowers. Drugs can be made from their seeds. These drugs can control pain.

Osiris

Hapi

Isis

Horus

Eye of Horus

Seth

a pharaoh with
a crook and flail

Anubis

canopic jars

Published by Macmillan Heinemann ELT
Between Towns Road, Oxford OX4 3PP
Macmillan Heinemann ELT is an imprint of
Macmillan Publishers Limited
Companies and representatives throughout the world
Heinemann is a registered trademark of Harcourt Education, used under licence.

ISBN 1–405073–05–5
EAN 978–1–405073–05–9

River God © Wilbur Smith 1993
First published by Macmillan 1993

This retold version by Stephen Colbourn for Macmillan Readers
First published 2002
Text © Macmillan Publishers Limited 2002, 2005
Design and illustration © Macmillan Publishers Limited 2002, 2005

This edition first published 2005

Designed by Sue Vaudin
Illustrated by Donald Harvey
Original cover template design by Jackie Hill
Cover illustration by Getty/Kenneth Garrett

Printed in Thailand

2009 2008 2007 2006 2005
10 9 8 7 6 5 4 3 2